D0551444

C155329650

"And you're a great believer in doing the decent thing?"

Was that her being coy? Flirting? Or what she felt passed for flirting, she amended silently. What was going on here?

She was both nervous and excited, even as she warned herself not to be.

"Whenever possible," he replied to her mocking question, fairly sure she was mocking him. He stole a glance at her now that they were relatively alone and unthreatened by traffic. "Whenever possible," he repeated.

Instead of feeling a sense of relief at his profession of honorability, her nerves instantly spiked even higher than before, fed by anticipation the magnitude of which she had never encountered before.

Just what did she think she was anticipating here? Cindy asked herself. Women were a dime a dozen for this man. Why would he bother singling her out?

And why did she so desperately want him to?

Dear Reader,

Welcome to the first installment of *The Kelley Legacy*, a family you first met in the pages of the last *The Coltons of Montana* miniseries.

We have a United States Senator who allowed his ever growing ego to lead him into regions a more prudent thinking man would have gone to great lengths to avoid. The purpose of the society he blundered into will be revealed slowly, but the chilling threat is evident immediately.

To the Senator's rescue comes his estranged son (one of six siblings), Dylan Kelley, a class A trial lawyer. He joins forces with the Senator's chief staff assistant, Cindy Jensen, who has secrets of her own. A challenge that will take a bit of work. But Dylan soon finds that Cindy is more than worth the extra effort he needs to put in.

As ever, I thank you for reading and from the bottom of my heart, I wish you someone to love who loves you back.

Marie Ferrarella

Private Justice

MARIE FERRARELLA

First published in Great Britain 2012
by Mills & Boon, an imprint of Harlequin (UK) Limited.
Large Print edition 2012
Harlequin (UK) Limited,
Eton House, 18-24 Paradise Road,
Richmond, Surrey TW9 1SR

© Harlequin Books S.A. 2011

ISBN: 978 0 263 22999 8

Special thanks and acknowledgment to Marie Ferrarella for her contribution to The Kelley Legacy miniseries.

Harlequin (UK) policy is to use papers that are natural, renewable and recyclable products and made from wood grown in sustainable forests. The logging and manufacturing process conform to the legal environmental regulations of the country of origin.

Printed and bound in Great Britain
by CPI Antony Rowe, Chippenham, Wiltshire

MARIE FERRARELLA

This bestselling and award-winning author has written more than two hundred books for Mills & Boon, some under the name Marie Nicole. Her romances are beloved by fans worldwide. Visit her website at www.marieferrarella.com

To
Kate Conrad,
a little fighter
if ever there was one.
Keep up the good fight.

Prologue

They were out there, waiting for him. Waiting to feed on his public humiliation.

Vultures!

The hairs on the back of Henry Thomas Kelley's neck stood on end as his anxiety grew.

He knew they were there before he even opened the courthouse door and walked out of the venerable building. Before he ever saw them, he sensed them. A gaggle of reporters clutching microphones as if they were weapons to be wielded, deadly weapons that, with the echo of one misplaced word, could kill all of a man's hopes, all his dreams. Kill everything he had built up over these long years.

Backed up by their cameramen, they were ready, willing and eager to record the downfall of what had been, just days before, a fairy-tale life—complete with a breathtaking, meteoric rise in the world of politics.

He'd been king of the world with no limit in sight. And now, now that he'd crossed the wrong people, expressed a hesitation where none had been anticipated or would be tolerated, the king, it appeared, was dead—and everyone wanted their chance to kick the corpse before it was dumped into an unmarked grave.

Hubris was a terrible thing, born of adulation and coming in on the backs of fawning lackeys. And Hank Kelley knew, to his shame, that he had been guilty of it. Been seduced by it. Everyone had wanted to be seen with him, be in his limelight. *Use* him.

And now, those same people were ready

to rend his body into tiny, indistinguishable pieces.

Joyfully.

He had been married to one of the richest women in the world, an attractive woman who had loved him, giving him five sons and a daughter. He and Sarah had been the absolutely perfect couple with the perfect family.

Had been.

And he had let it all go to his head.

He had stopped deflecting the flattering attentions of all those beautiful women who seemingly wanted nothing more than to be with him. To *love* him.

Vain, flattered, he'd stopped resisting, and the trap, he now realized, had been set. A trap to be used against him whenever it was deemed necessary by the people he'd so naively trusted.

Apparently, now it was necessary.

Now, not one, not two, but six of the women he'd been involved with—calling themselves mistresses when that title hardly fitted—all tall, all willowy, all blondes, had stepped forward to point an accusing finger at the man they were all claiming had seduced them.

It had been the other way around. It was *always* the other way around. But the end result was the same. He had cheated. Cheated on the wife who had loved him, cheated on the public who had trusted him, and that was all the public cared about.

That and watching his public humiliation, his public fall from grace.

It made for a great show.

Taking in one long breath, Hank braced himself and pushed open the door. He would have lowered his head to avoid looking at them, but it would have been taken as an act of cowardice, and he might be many things, but a coward was not one of them.

With determined steps he began to make his

way to his waiting vehicle, enduring a hail of questions that swelled into a storm of noise.

"Senator, Senator! Look this way!"

"This way!"

"Are you the father of that woman's baby?" Someone shouted the soul-scraping question louder than her fellow reporters.

His mouth, so often seen with a radiant smile, was grim. He kept his eyes on his target, the car, and avoided making any eye contact with the swarm around him, no matter how tightly they closed in around him.

He pushed forward.

"No comment," he finally bit off as the questions grew and multiplied, choking the very air around him. He was beginning to doubt he was going to make it to his car in one piece. It couldn't end like this. Not here. Not before he found a way to apologize to Sarah for the grief he had caused her. He had never meant to hurt her. He just didn't think.

He kept plowing his way through the human throng, making progress by inches. He needed not only to get away, but to find somewhere he could go and think. What was happening was not a coincidence.

But why now? Why this?

He needed answers.

After what felt like an eternity embroiled in an endless journey, he finally made it to his car. The driver, Joseph, was standing holding the rear door open for him, waiting. He was quickly ushered in, his useless lawyer diving in right behind him, and the door was secured.

Exhausted, relieved, he leaned back and exhaled a sigh filled with anxiety.

"Where to, sir?" Joseph asked after sliding into the driver's seat and slamming the door.

Both sides of the somber, black customized vehicle were besieged by the relentless reporters, still trying to get a sound bite, a single damning word.

"Anywhere," Hank cried. "Just away from here."

The car was already in motion, burrowing through the throng. "You got it, Senator."

"Damn fool idiot!"

Bonnie Gene Kelley was walking by the den where her husband of forty years, Donald, could occasionally be found when he wasn't up to his elbows in yet another barbecue sauce, trying to create one to top the one he'd breathed life into the time before. All created to be used at his very successful chain of steak houses.

The sound of Donald's voice stopped her in her tracks and she peered in.

"Talking to yourself again, dear?" she asked. It was getting to be an unfortunate habit, she thought. People were going to think he was losing his mental faculties if he wasn't careful. "You know, if you want some company," she told him, walking into the room, "all you have to do is ask."

Donald continued scowling at the TV.

Glancing toward the flat screen, she asked, "What are you watching?" before she had a chance to focus on the face of the man on the monitor.

Her eyes widened. *Oh my God!*

"Donald, is that Hank?" she cried, completely stunned.

Donald was still communing with the image on the screen. "Damn *stupid* idiot," Donald retorted angrily. With a snap of his wrist, he made the picture disappear, shutting off the set just as the words *recorded earlier* scrolled across the bottom of the screen. "He never could keep from messing up a good thing!"

"Donald, why was Hank in the middle of that ugly crowd? Is something wrong? Why was he on the news?"

Bonnie Gene turned toward her husband, expecting him to give her an answer or at least to share in her confusion as to why Hank was the subject of a news story.

Donald didn't want to talk about it. Not yet. Not until he got his temper under control.

Shaking his head, his asymmetrically cut, shaggy white hair—that he insisted only *she* cut—moving about independently, he acted as if he hadn't heard any of her questions and announced, "I'm going back to the restaurant. That barbecue sauce isn't going to create itself."

"Donald," Bonnie Gene cried, raising her voice as he strode past her to the den's threshold, "talk to me."

"That *was* talking, Bonnie Gene," Donald said as he walked out. "Thought someone who's always doing it would recognize it when she heard it." He didn't bother turning around.

Bonnie Gene, frowning, picked up the remote and turned the set back on. But the news had moved on and cut to a commercial. A bright, smiling blonde with way too many teeth was extolling the virtues of her shampoo.

Disgusted, Bonnie Gene turned off the set again and, with an annoyed sigh, left the room, promising herself that she was going to get the information out of her husband when he came home for the night. She wanted to know what was going on. The senator from California, Hank Kelley, was Donald's younger and, for all intents and purposes, estranged half brother. But family was family and she intended to get to the bottom of this.

Donald, she thought, had better come clean if he knew what was good for him.

Chapter 1

Just when I thought there were no surprises left when it came to you, you had to show me I was wrong, didn't you, Dad?

Several states away, in a prestigious law firm in Beverly Hills, California, high-powered attorney Dylan Kelley was watching the same news broadcast as his much-loved uncle Donald.

Biting off a curse, Dylan aimed his remote at the huge flat-screen TV on the opposite wall and terminated the broadcast. The screen went to black and, for a moment, silence ensued.

Dylan shook his head in dazed disbelief. So much for his father's straight-arrow image.

"You really outdid yourself this time, Dad," he muttered under his breath, anger beginning to set in and take a firm hold.

He wondered if either of his brothers or his sister, Lana, knew about this latest turn of events. Worse, what if his mother had caught this bulletin? She was a strong woman, a woman who had, over the years, slowly constructed walls and barriers around herself. He'd been a witness to that, watching the walls as they came up, holding her in.

Holding everyone else out.

He realized now, as an adult, that she'd done it to protect herself against being hurt. As if she somehow knew that this was in the offing.

Had she suspected? Did she know? He felt incredibly bad for her, incredibly angry at his absentee father for having done this to her.

Dylan sighed, sitting back down at his desk

for a moment. For just a split second, his knees felt weak. If he felt like this, how must his mother feel?

Just goes to show you, he thought. Fairy tales were just that, fairy tales. They had no bearing on real life. The press and people in general had called his parents' marriage a real-life, magical fairy-tale. Years ago, he'd stumbled across an old article in a magazine, an interview with his father written when Hank had just been starting out on his political rise—his eye even then on a very lofty prize.

His father had freely admitted, apparently with pride, that he had married an exceedingly rich woman who supported him in every way, eager to make him happy, eager to give him his heart's desire, no matter what it was. Along the way, she'd also given him the perfect photo op family.

Dylan took in a deep breath as he closed his eyes and remembered being trotted out with his brothers and baby sister, all perfectly groomed, him wearing a suit he'd hated at the time, to stand around his father and mother, big smiles pasted on all their faces for the camera that froze their supposed happiness forever in time.

Or at least long enough to generate a favorable impression with the voting public. His father had been the family-values candidate.

He wondered if his father saw the irony in that now.

Agitated, Dylan dragged his hand through his thick, dark hair, remembering that the creation of those family portraits provided almost the only occasions when he actually got to see his father. The rest of the time, Hank was busy traveling, glad-handing potential constituents up and down the length and breadth of California, professing his undying willingness to work until he dropped for the good of the people of "this glorious, sun-kissed state of ours."

And the voters had believed him. Believed every single word. They'd sent his father to the United States Senate, confident that he would represent them to the best of his ability, which was definitely good enough for them.

Who his father wound up representing, apparently, was himself, Dylan thought darkly, his mind going back to the jarring news story expounding on the fact that his father was being investigated on charges of illegal activities and criminal misuse of campaign funds.

One of the newscasters, looking properly shocked, said that there were allegations the missing campaign funds had been spent on setting up his mistresses, one of whom was said to be currently pregnant.

Mistresses.

Damn it, Dad, what the hell were you thinking? Didn't you just once think about this getting out and hurting Mom? Dylan demanded silently.

He hadn't seen his father in—what? Six months? A year? More?

He'd lost track. The last few times he had been the one to seek out his father, who never just showed up to see how his son was doing or how life was going for the family in general. His father was always too busy to take the time to stay in touch.

And now I know what you apparently were too busy with, Dylan thought angrily.

Well, if the prosecutors had their way, he was still going to have to go to his father in order to see him. And this time it would be because his father was incarcerated.

How the mighty have fallen.

"What the hell were you thinking?" he repeated, this time out loud, addressing a man who was not there.

Who hadn't been there, even when he *was,* for a long, long time.

Dylan looked at the framed photograph on

his desk. A photograph of the whole family taken for a Christmas card some four years ago. His eyes narrowed as he focused on the handsome older man in the center—his father's usual position.

"If I had half a brain, I'd just let you stew in your own juices and go on with my life. Just like you'd do for me and the others if we needed you." He had no doubt of that. What little fatherly love Henry Kelley had available went to Lana, because she was the youngest and the only girl.

And Lana had always worshipped him and defended him, no matter what. God only knew why.

Lana could probably find a reason to defend their father now, Dylan thought.

He leaned back in his chair, rocking slightly, thinking. If he went with his first inclination, if he just continued with his life and did nothing, in effect, he would be no better than the man who had earned his disdain.

Worse, because he knew better, knew how this kind of behavior affected the person on the receiving end. Ultimately, if he turned his back on his father now, he'd somehow wind up hurting his mother, who still, he suspected, deep down in her patrician heart, loved his father no matter what. She was that kind of a person, even though she tried not to show it.

Dylan frowned. When the final analysis was in and all was said and done, blood was thicker than water and that still meant something to him, if not to his father.

But he wasn't going to do this for his father. He was going to do it for his mother. And also to prove to himself that he was a better man than his father apparently was.

Added to that, Dylan thought as he began to throw a few things into his briefcase and get ready to go to his father's Beverly Hills office, the family reputation was at stake here. He had no doubt that if his father went down, the stain would mark all of them.

It didn't matter that the rest of the family had little or no interaction with the man. The shame of his conviction, if it came to that, would be something they would all have to bear. And while his father might have done things to merit the ostracization, he, his brothers and sister and especially his mother, had not.

"You really don't deserve anyone in the family coming to your aid, old man," Dylan muttered under his breath as he left his office. "You really don't."

But he knew he was bound to do it anyway.

If this was fifty years ago—and a romantic comedy, Cindy Jensen added cynically—she would have been referred to as a Girl Friday.

"As well as a Girl Saturday, Sunday, Monday, Tuesday, Wednesday and Thursday," she said out loud.

However, in this modern world, the official title she bore was Chief Staff Assistant to Senator Henry Thomas Kelley. In reality, she was far more than that. She was his confidante, his mother, his cheerleader, his secretary. In effect, his walking, talking point of reference for almost everything under the sun, plus his gofer and, last but not least, his general smoother-outer of ruffled feathers.

She did a far better job of it than the pretentious fool the senator had hired as his press secretary, she thought grudgingly.

Too bad that with all those various job descriptions she hadn't found a way to be his private conscience as well, because, Lord knew, as she had found out a couple of days ago, the man certainly needed one.

Desperately.

While she believed very strongly in his political agenda—if she hadn't, she wouldn't have been here, wouldn't have given her all to work her way up his team—she absolutely hated this other side of him. The side she'd unwillingly had confirmed for her via a news bulletin. The side that, in truth, she had come to suspect whenever the senator had asked her to clear some time for him from his calendar and been more than a little evasive whenever she'd asked him why he needed that time cleared for him. He'd mutter something about having an appointment he couldn't break and flash that thousand-watt smile of his, once again charming his way out of the situation.

Well, his charm had certainly failed the man this time, she thought.

Feet of clay. That was the term for it, she recalled. The family-values crusader had feet of clay.

The realization cut through her like a knife.

The phone on his desk rang again for the

umpteenth time. It had been ringing off the hook all morning, ever since the story had broken about the senator having to go to the L.A. courthouse regarding an investigation into his campaign funds, and suddenly mistresses—*mistresses* of all things!—had begun crawling out of the woodwork.

Ever since that bulletin had burst on her, her tiny, optimistic visions of this world the senator inhabited and she was working toward promoting had been crushed.

God knew she had few enough optimistic things to cling to. Her private life, well, that was a complete washout, but she had clung to her professional life, viewing it as her one saving grace, telling herself that at least what she was doing had merit for the country and she was going to have to find comfort—and ultimately validation—in that. She sure knew she wasn't going to find it on the home front, not with the bastard in designer suits she'd had the misfortune to fall in love with and marry.

No, she hadn't fallen in love with *him,* she'd fallen in love with the image he'd projected. Fallen in love with a man who didn't exist. The one who *did* exist had had a foul temper and swinging fists. Fists that, she was ashamed to admit even to herself, had made contact. And she had taken it. In the beginning.

But after a spate of time when she'd blamed herself for causing his outbursts—just as he blamed her—she'd come to her senses. She'd realized that *none* of this—his outbursts, his out-of-control temper, his reasons for losing it—none of it was her fault. That was when, with the senator's support, she had called the police.

It had been the first step in reclaiming her life, her very soul. And except for the curve she'd discovered she'd been thrown, a curve she now lived with every day, she pretty much *had* reclaimed it. Reclaimed it by throwing herself into her work, striving to make Senator Henry William Kelley the next popular candidate for the presidency of the United States.

It had seemed only right, because he'd been there to take her side, to encourage her not to allow her ex, Dean, to mistreat her. The senator had been the father she'd never really known.

And now this.

It was safe to say that the senator's chances of gaining the presidency had pretty much been blown to hell. Much the way her faith in him had been.

Damn, it just wasn't fair! Just how blind could she have been to miss this red flag? How deluded was her state of mind to see a hero where an old-fashioned scoundrel stood?

How could he? How *could* he?

"This can't take away from what he's accomplished, Cindy, it can't," she told herself fiercely, conducting an argument that was mostly in her head.

The man was still a good senator, still a man who had the interest of his country foremost in his heart, if not his mind. Still the man who had helped her. She had to remember that. Moreover, she had to do her best to remind the public of all his good points.

Just because it had been discovered that the senator had the personal morals of an alley cat didn't mean that he couldn't do great things for the people who voted for him.

"But it sure does rock the boat," she ground out angrily.

The next moment she jumped as the door opened. She'd left orders not to be disturbed because she had damage control to do.

Who was ignoring her instructions?

And then she had her answer. Kind of.

A tall, well-groomed and quite handsome man who looked to be in his early thirties walked into the senator's office. His chiseled features were complemented by straight, dark hair, worn slightly long, and his piercing, intelligent blue eyes.

Here was a man who got by on his looks first, then made use of anything he had in his arsenal—if necessary, she thought.

Well, whatever he did, he could do it somewhere else. He was trespassing as far as she was concerned.

"You're not supposed to be here," she snapped at him angrily, recovering from her initial surprise.

Dylan looked around. Was she the only one in the office?

"I heard you talking to someone," he said.

She stared at him. It almost sounded like an accusation, Cindy thought. Who the hell did he think he was?

"Even if I were, that doesn't give you an excuse for barging in," she informed him, expecting him to offer some apology and then leave.

He did neither. Instead, he remained standing where he was, looking around the office again, as if he expected someone to pop out of the shadows.

Dylan scanned the office more slowly this time, taking in what he'd missed at first glance. The pretty young woman with the pinned-back, golden-brown hair and the damning dark-brown eyes was still the only one here.

"Where is he?" Dylan asked the attractive watchdog. "The senator," he clarified, even though he had a feeling there was no need to.

Her hands were on her hips, the picture of barely suppressed fury. "He's not here."

"But you were just talking to him." She hadn't been on the phone when he walked in, so he couldn't have interrupted a phone conversation. That meant that the woman had been talking to someone in the room. Since this was his father's office, where had he gone?

Her eyes—rather attractive eyes, he noted—narrowed into piercing slits. "I was talking to myself, if it's any business of yours," she said curtly.

Nodding, he accepted the explanation. But he had a pressing question that needed answering. "Okay, where is he?"

Well, that gave her the identity of the mystery stranger, or at least told her his occupation. Her hackles went up.

"Can't you damn reporters leave him alone? Aren't you going to be satisfied until you're chewing on his bones? Even if I knew," she ended defiantly, "I wouldn't tell you."

She was lying, Dylan thought. There was something in her eyes that told him she knew exactly where the "good senator" was. She was covering for his father. Was there more than just professional loyalty at play here? He looked at her more closely.

His eyes swept over her and he took a *really* good look at the woman standing before him like a member of the emperor's royal guard.

The woman wasn't just pretty, she was damn attractive, bordering on downright gorgeous. She wasn't his father's usual type—the woman had honey-brown hair, not blond, and her eyes, instead of the usual blue, were the color of an inviting, cool root beer on a hot day. But who knew? Maybe the old man was branching out in his lechery. He certainly wouldn't put it—or anything else—past his father. Not after that news story had knocked the pins out from under him, Dylan thought.

"Are you one of my father's…friends?" he asked the woman tactfully.

There'd been a long, significant pause between the last two words. Pregnant enough to make her eyes blaze and her temper flare.

"What I am, if it's any of your business," Cindy snapped, indignantly drawing herself up to her full five-foot-four, "is the senator's Chief Staff Assist—wait." She came to a sudden, skidding halt as her eyes widened and she stared at him. "Did you just say 'my father?'"

"Actually, I said 'my father's,'" he corrected glibly. "But, for the record, you got the general gist of it."

For the moment, she took no note of the sarcasm. "You're the senator's son," she said incredulously.

"Yes." Why did the woman look so surprised at that? Though they were estranged, it wasn't as if his father kept his family a secret.

Not like his mistresses, Dylan's mind added tersely.

How did she even know that this was the senator's son? Cindy thought. For all she knew, this tall man in a designer suit was a reporter—apparently a good one if the cut of his expensive clothes was any indication. And the man was trying to talk—to lie, she amended—his way in here.

"Why haven't I seen you before?" she challenged.

"Maybe because the good senator's not being very fatherly these days now that he doesn't need his wife and family for photo ops." He fixed the woman with a look that he'd used to take witnesses—and courtroom opponents— down a peg. "I haven't seen you, either, and yet I'm willing to believe that you're his—what was it you called it again? Chief Staff Assistant?"

She didn't like the way his mouth curved when he said that. Didn't like his tone and she *definitely* didn't like the way his eyes swept over her, as if he was taking the measure of a thing, not an actual person. She'd had more than enough of that kind of treatment from her ex-may-he-roast-on-a-flaming-spit-husband.

Her chin went up in an automatic, reflexive move at the same time that her eyes narrowed again.

"Yes," she ground out. "I'm Senator Henry Thomas Kelley's Chief Staff Assistant, and if you are actually the senator's son, I'd like some proof, please."

His father obviously liked them feisty, Dylan thought, taking out his wallet, not doubting for a moment that while this woman might really be what she claimed to be, she was also one of the growing number of mistresses. In his opinion, she was an infinitely better choice than the three women whose faces had been flashed across the screen during the unsettling news story.

He flipped his wallet open to his driver's license and held it out to her.

Waiting a beat for her to read it, he asked, "Proof enough? Or would you also like to fingerprint me?" As she pushed back his wallet, he flipped it closed again and slipped it back into his pocket. "You can check my prints against the ones on file with the California Bar Association if you really want to be thorough." Straightening his jacket, he added, "I could also leave you a sample of my blood if it suits your fancy."

"No need to get sarcastic," she informed him stiffly. He was the man's son all right. Now that she thought of it, she should have seen the family resemblance in his features. It was just that she was too angry to think clearly right now. "It's been completely insane here the last couple of days."

As if to back up her point, the phone abruptly started ringing again. She picked up the receiver and then dropped it back into the cradle without stopping to see who was on the other end or even breaking her verbal stride.

"I've had reporters all but climbing up the side of the building to gain access to the senator's office. They're like vultures circling, looking for a way to swoop by and get their piece of flesh."

"Sounds like you have your hands full," he commented with a trace of sympathy.

"This isn't—" Another call came in and she repeated her movements from a moment ago, lifting and then dropping the receiver into the phone's cradle, this time a little more sharply than the last. "—what I signed on for," she concluded.

It did sound like a zoo in here, he thought. The sooner he got his information, the sooner he would be able to leave. "*Do* you know where my father is?" Dylan asked again.

"If the two of you have been so out of touch," Cindy pointed out, "why do you want to know where he is?" Another phone call had her losing her temper and she disconnected the phone from the jack in the wall.

Decisive woman, he thought. "Because the

senator needs help, and right now, I might be one of the few people interested in actually getting him out of this hole he's dug for himself."

She wasn't buying this so easily, Cindy thought. "Because you love him so much."

"So pretty and yet so cynical." He laughed, shaking his head. "No, not because I love him so much. Because he's my father, and the bottom line is, much as I might think he deserves it, I don't want to see him torn apart in public. If anyone's going to tear him apart, it'll be me and it'll be in private," he concluded. "Now, do you or don't you know where my father is hiding out?" he asked one last time, looking at her pointedly.

Chapter 2

Cindy looked at the senator's son for a long moment, not saying anything, not volunteering the information he was asking for. But there was a reason for that. She was not one to be cowed by an authoritative voice, at least, not anymore. And not ever again.

"How do I know you're going to do what you say you're going to do, Mr. Kelley?" she challenged.

Miss Warmth-and-Charm had lost him. He wondered if everyone who worked in the realm of politics eventually became proficient in a form of double-talk through diligent practice, or if it just came naturally to some, that in turn led them to believe they had a future in the political arena.

"Run that by me again," Dylan requested.

Okay, she'd approach it differently, Cindy thought. "You're saying you want to help the senator."

Wasn't that what he'd just told her? "Yes, that's the general idea."

And he wasn't going to do it by standing around in his father's Beverly Hills office if the man wasn't to be found in it as well, Dylan thought impatiently. At this point, it would take very little for him to throw his hands up and walk away from the whole thing. He hadn't wanted to be involved in the first place, and if he had to jump through hoops, well, that was asking a bit too much in his opinion.

Rather than immediately volunteering an address, his father's petite guard dog engaged him in another annoying round of rhetoric.

"How do I know that's true? How do I know you're not going to take the information I give you and sell it to the highest tabloid bidder just to get even with the senator?" she wanted to know, assuming, for the sake of argument, that this man was in a bad way when it came to finances and was doing it for the money. For all she knew, the designer suit he was wearing could have been a gift—or borrowed. "By your own admission, your father-son relationship is far from the kind of stuff that they like to immortalize in myopic memoirs."

He stared at her. Well, that certainly was a mouthful. There was no way anyone would get her confused with an empty-headed bimbo, which, he'd come to learn extremely quickly, was what his father's mistresses all had in common. Beyond their glamorous, carbon-copy looks, they all had the IQs of dormant peanuts. Maybe his father had decided to add

an intelligent one to the body count for variety's sake.

"So what you're telling me is," Dylan said,
just to make sure he understood what she was
saying, "barring some kind of divine intervention, you're not going to give me the address
of his 'safe house.'"

Her smile was tight. "Finally," her eyes
seemed to say. "That's what I'm telling you."

Okay, if she wanted divine intervention, there
was only one way to go. He might not be on
a first-name basis with God, but he was, so to
speak, with his father. And, he had a hunch
that in this case, a word from his almighty father would have the same effect on this overly
protective woman.

"Could you at least call my father and let me
talk to him?" Dylan requested, doing his best
to sound patient. "We can let him decide."

Cindy paused, thinking. The man standing
before her did seem sincere, but that was ob-

viously something that, whether he liked it or not, this bright young lawyer had inherited from his father. The senator was the type of man who could persuade a survivor of the *Titanic* to book a three-week cruise to Alaska and make the person believe it was his own idea. She'd never met anyone so convincing.

It apparently ran in the family. But she had had her shots, thanks to her ex, and it took a great deal to sway her from her position once she took it.

Determined to get this woman to come around, Dylan tried again. "Look, wouldn't you hold yourself accountable if you do keep us apart and the senator winds up getting nailed to the cross for his transgressions?" On his way over to the office, he had done a little calling around to various sources. The picture that had emerged of his father's immediate future did *not* look good. "Right now, everyone thinks he's guilty of everything, including starting both world wars. If I don't at least *try* to help him, there's no telling where this is going to end up." He pinned her with a penetrating look. "You want that on your conscience?"

This time, the silence was a great deal shorter. "You're good," she told him grudgingly when she spoke. "I will give you that."

"What I am," he countered, "is right. Now, what'll it be? The new address, his phone number or an eternally guilty conscience?" He laid out her three choices and waited.

"You know, there is always the possibility that the public will come to their senses, the investigation will find him not guilty of misappropriation of campaign funds and those women will all admit to lying for the purposes of blackmail." She looked at him. He was the personification of skepticism. "You've got to admit that's a possibility."

He congratulated himself on not laughing in her face. Talk about a cockeyed optimist. He wouldn't have thought it of her, not after first seeing the other side of the woman.

"Sure it is. Right after pigs fly. They'll not only fly," he added, "but they'll have their pilots' licenses, pilots' jackets with little gold wings pinned over the pockets and they'll all be speaking French. Fluently," he concluded.

He was mocking her, she thought angrily. Why was it all the good-looking men thought they had a God-given right to put everyone else down and act as if they were the only ones who mattered? The only ones who were allowed to have an opinion—and that opinion was always right.

Her eyes pinned him. "You're a pessimist, I take it."

Actually, he saw himself as the reverse in most cases. But in this case, it was neither. "What I am is a pragmatic man who is trying to help the head of his family save face and not go down for the things he hasn't done, however little that might turn out to be. Now, for the last time, can you at least give me his phone number and let me talk to the man before it's too late?"

She didn't like the way this man kept refusing to refer to the senator by his title, but used either a pronoun or something equally as anonymous. To her, that was a sign of how little he thought of his father. She still couldn't reconcile the notion that he was willing to go out of his way like this for someone he held in such contempt. *Was* there an angle he was going for that she was missing?

In any event, though she hated to admit it, he was right. The least she could do was give him that phone number he'd asked for. The final decision about a face-to-face meeting ultimately had to lie with the senator. She was not about to presume to speak on his behalf. All she could do was lay the groundwork and make sure that no reporters got to Senator Kelley.

Exhaling loudly as if the act would bring her very lungs out, Cindy capitulated. She pulled a notepad closer to her on the desk and wrote out a telephone number. Finished, she pushed the pad toward him.

Dylan looked at it. It was an 818 area code, but that didn't mean anything. This was the number to his father's cell phone; his father could be anywhere in the state. Or out of it. *Nobody said this was going to be easy,* he thought with resignation.

Tearing the sheet off the pad, he said, "By the way, you know my name because it was on my license, but I don't know yours."

She didn't take the opening he gave her. "No, you don't."

This was like pulling teeth. *Or, actually, more like questioning a hostile witness under oath,* he thought. "What is it?" he asked her.

There was pure suspicion in her eyes. "Why, so you can have me investigated?"

"So I know what to call you when I need to get your attention."

"Through," Cindy told him without missing a beat.

The corners of his mouth curved slightly. "First or last?"

Cindy cocked her head. "Excuse me?"

"Through," he repeated what she'd just said to him. "Is that your first name or your last name?"

He was a lawyer all right, Cindy thought. One who wasn't going to stop badgering her until he got what he was after. Well, she supposed that it was an easy enough matter for him to find out the name of the senator's Chief Staff Assistant. She might as well tell him now rather than keep the game going.

"Cindy," she told him grudgingly. "Cindy Jensen."

That hadn't taken as long as he'd begun to think it would. His smile was broad. "Nice to meet you Cindy, Cindy Jensen."

"You know," she told him, "you'd get along a lot better with people if you lost that mocking tone."

Now *that* amused him. "*You're* giving me advice on how to get along with people?" Didn't that fall into the realm of the pot-and-kettle thing?

She took offense at his response and what it implied. "I'll have you know I get along beautifully with people. Non-belligerent people," she qualified.

"I only act belligerently with people who are trying to stonewall me." He looked at the phone number in his hand. "Now that you've given me a number where my father can be reached, we can become best friends."

Her response was immediate and without hesitation. "I'd rather eat dirt."

"Odd choice," he commented, keeping a straight face even though he knew he was goading her, "but I won't stand in your way. Whatever makes you happy."

"What would make me happy," Cindy said under her breath as she resumed moving about the office, straightening things up just so that her hands could remain busy, "is if the senator had remembered to stay a little truer to his own principles and not done anything to allow the media the opportunity to jump on his bones like a pack of snarling jackals."

Dylan had started dialing, but stopped to listen to her. Her tone had dropped and her voice had softened. Her imagery entertained him.

"Anyone ever tell you that you're a very colorful woman?" She gave him a look that told him she was not about to be softened up with compliments. "I guess not," he concluded.

About to continue dialing, he winced as a piercing noise was emitted from the earpiece of the receiver and a female, almost metallic voice, came on the line, reciting the classic instruction: "Please hang up and dial again."

He was about to press down the button on the cradle when Cindy did it for him. He raised his eyes to hers, thinking she'd obviously heard the jarring message. "Thanks."

She gave him an ever-so-slight nod of the head to acknowledge that she had heard him.

As he completed dialing the number, Dylan couldn't help wondering what it was like to have someone who was as loyal to him as this woman apparently was to his father. His first thought was that his father had to be paying her awfully well. But money didn't buy loyalty, it bought lackeys, and a couple of minutes in Cindy Jensen's company had convinced him that this woman was no lackey. So then what was she? The senator's Chief Staff Assistant/ head mistress? Or what?

He was going to need to get that cleared up

in order to have a handle on the facts here. And on what was and wasn't, ultimately, a press liability. Because he knew just as well as anyone that cases were first tried in the press. A victory there gave a victory elsewhere a base to grow from, becoming that much easier to achieve.

God knew he was going to have his work cut out for him.

He blew out an impatient breath. The phone had rung now a total of eight times and there'd been no answer, human or machine. In this day and age, that was pretty unusual in his book. Was she giving him the runaround again?

Dylan looked at her. "You sure this is the right number?"

She didn't like the veiled accusation in his voice. "It's the contact number that the senator gave me," she told him.

Dylan frowned, debating hanging up. If there *was* someone there, how long could they put up with listening to the phone ring? He had his suspicions that it was a bogus number— unless his father was out, and considering the high visibility of his face after the broadcast, he sincerely doubted that.

Of course, there was also another explanation for why no one was picking up. One that absolved the Chief Staff Assistant of any blame.

"How much does my father trust you?" he asked her suddenly.

Cindy stopped moving around the office, stopped neatening, stopped straightening. She slowly turned around to look at him. Just what was this lawyer who might or might not have pure intentions saying?

"I'm the senator's Chief Staff Assist—"

Dylan raised his hand to stop her in midword. This refrain was beginning to sound like a broken record and it was grating on his nerves. "Yes, yes, I know. You're his Chief

Staff Assistant. You told me. Trust me, you *told* me."

Two could take that sarcastic tone, she thought, annoyed. "And you remembered. How nice for you." The words were delivered with a smile that could have frozen a pond in July.

The woman definitely had an attitude problem, but that was something he'd deal with later. Right now, he needed to find a way to get to his damn father. The old man had picked a hell of a time for a game of hide and seek.

"You being his Chief Staff Assistant doesn't automatically mean that he trusts you," he pointed out, less than tactfully. "Maybe he gave you that number to throw you off."

With a disgusted noise, Dylan hung up the phone. Now what? He supposed he could go back to his firm and see if the private investigator they kept on retainer could locate his father.

Her eyes all but shooting daggers at him,

Cindy crossed back to the desk and elbowed him aside.

"Give me that," she said, commandeering the phone and pulling the receiver out of his hand. On a hunch, she hit the redial button, then watched the caller ID screen as the numbers of the phone call he'd just made popped up one by one. Just as she'd thought. "No wonder," she declared. Cindy raised her eyes to his face, a look of triumph on her own.

What was she up to? "No wonder what?" he wanted to know.

The phone on the other end began ringing. For a moment, she ignored it as she pointed to the screen for his benefit. "You transposed two of the numbers."

Terminating the call, Cindy tapped in the right numbers on the keypad and then listened as the phone on the other end began to ring.

Dylan silently upbraided himself for the mistake. That was careless. And he'd been so careful lately, too. It hadn't happened to him in a number of years now. Most days, when he remembered not to rush himself, he could keep the dyslexia completely under control.

No one at the firm suspected he had it. And except for this one girl—and he'd never confirmed it, saying she had to be mistaken— no one in either his college or the law school he'd subsequently attended, had ever even suspected that he had it.

It was, overall, rather a mild form of the annoying condition. But it was always there, in the shadows, waiting to bedevil him when he least expected it, if he just let his guard down. And it always appeared when he had the least amount of time to deal with it.

Until just now, it hadn't cropped up for a very long time. He'd begun to think that maybe he was finally free of it. Finally free to feel unencumbered.

Just went to show him he was going to have to remain ever-diligent and on his guard.

He supposed that there were a lot worse things in life.

Like a father courting public scandal.

"Anyone?" he asked his father's Chief Staff Assistant as she held the phone against her ear.

Rather than answer him, Cindy held the receiver out for him to take. The ringing noise had ceased. A deep, masculine voice on the other end was saying, "Hello? Hello? Is anyone there?"

Dylan grabbed the receiver from her and placed it against his ear. It sounded like his father, but he couldn't be sure.

"Dad? Dad, is that you?"

For a moment, there was silence on the other end. It stretched out so long that Dylan thought perhaps the connection had been lost. Or maybe the man on the other end had just laid the phone down and walked away. That, in his opinion, would have been par for the course, representing the sort of behavior he had come to expect from his father.

And then, just as he was about to hang up the receiver, the same voice cautiously asked, "Who is this?"

It made sense that his father didn't immediately recognize his voice, Dylan decided. After all, it wasn't as if they spent hours on the phone, talking. Or any time at all, really. When it came right down to it, other than a few calls home from his father over the years, he couldn't remember ever talking to him on the phone.

Phoning to catch up was just not his father's way. These days, he seemed to like his family subdued and out of sight.

Too bad you can't follow your own required behavior, Dad.

"This is Dylan Kelley," he answered, then added, "your son," for good measure.

The information was met with more silence on the other end.

Chapter 3

Just as he was about to surrender his last shred of patience and say something really terse to his father, Dylan heard the voice on the other end of the line challenge, "How do I know that you are who you say you are? How do I know that it's really you?"

He didn't remember his father being this paranoid. But then, his personal memories of his father were admittedly not only few and far in between, but vague as well.

"Why?" Dylan asked. "You have another son named Dylan?"

"No, but my son Dylan hasn't spoken to me

in months now. So many that I can't really re-call just how long," his father replied.

It annoyed Dylan that his father made his answer sound more like an accusation than a statement of a situation that he had brought upon himself. "And I wouldn't be calling now if you hadn't gotten yourself into one hell of a mess."

Hank was still wary. Still nervous. "My son wouldn't care."

"I don't," Dylan answered coldly. "But all of this is ripping the hell out of Mother."

The last he'd heard, his mother had gone into hiding to avoid having to make any sort of a statement or subject herself to the public's in-satiable appetite for scandal.

For a split second, Dylan debated continu-ing on this path. Inadvertently, his father was handing him his way out. He could just back away, saying something inane about just wanting to check on his father's whereabouts and now that he had, he was done with it.

But that wasn't why he was here, Dylan reminded himself stoically. He was here not just to do damage control but, like it or not, to try to pull his father out of this quagmire.

"I'm offering you my services so we can find a way out of this and spare Mother any further humiliation. After everything you've put her through, essentially leaving her to raise the four of us by herself, she doesn't deserve this." And if it hadn't been for his uncle Donald, they would have found themselves to be all alone. The nannies and servants were exceedingly poor substitutes for a parent's love, a parent's attention. "The press is hell-bent on hounding her."

He heard his father laugh shortly. "I know the feeling."

Dylan knew he should keep his comment to himself, but he just couldn't. There was a deep-seated anger he needed to vent before he could be of any use to the old man. "I doubt that you're able to feel anything at all that doesn't directly affect you."

There was a pause again. He was sincerely skeptical that guilt had backed his father into silence. When it came to what the family thought of him, Dylan was convinced that his father had the emotional hide of a rhino.

When the senator spoke again, it was to ask another question. "How did you get this number?"

Dylan glanced toward the woman who had given up all pretense of not paying attention to every word he was saying. She stood on the other side of the desk, unabashedly listening to his end of the conversation, most likely trying to fill in the blanks that she wasn't able to hear.

"Your Chief Staff Assistant gave it to me."

"Cindy Jensen gave it to you?" his father asked incredulously. "She believed you?"

Dylan sighed. He hadn't come here to play games. His time was too precious for that. Hitting the speaker button, he retired the receiver into the cradle. "Here, why don't you ask her yourself? I just put you on speakerphone."

"Where are you?" Hank wanted to know, far from won over.

"I'm standing in your Beverly Hills office," Dylan told him. And then he turned his attention to Cindy. "Ball's in your court, Chief Staff Assistant," he said, deliberately putting emphasize on the word *chief.*

"Cindy?" Hank asked uncertainly.

"I'm right here, Senator," Cindy answered, moving closer to the phone on the desk.

"Cindy." There was relief in Hank's voice, as if he could now relax because someone he trusted—one of the few individuals he trusted—was there on his behalf. "And you're convinced that you're dealing with my son?

One of my sons?" Hank said, qualifying his question.

"Yes, sir," Cindy replied firmly. "He showed me his driver's license."

"Driver's licenses can be faked," Hank pointed out, then instructed her to describe him.

Cindy frowned. She hadn't thought of that, that the man could be showing her a fake driver's license. Her eyes narrowed as she looked at the individual on the other side of the desk more closely. Something in her gut told her she was right, despite the momentary uncertainty.

"He's about six foot one," she began.

"Six foot two and a half," Dylan corrected her. It wasn't that the inch and a half difference was so important, he just wanted her to be accurate. He knew damn well that his father had absolutely no idea how tall he actually was.

Cindy ignored Dylan's interjection. "He's got intense blue eyes and really thick dark hair."

She paused for a second, weighing her next sentence before continuing. "He could stand a haircut," she commented.

He'd gotten nothing but positive responses from the women in his office and the ones he went out with. Obviously this one liked to go against the grain. "I like it this length," Dylan informed her.

Cindy responded with a careless shrug of her slim shoulders, then went on as if he hadn't said anything. "But he dresses well. And if I look at him from the side," which she did now, moving to another vantage point around the desk, "he looks a little like a younger version of you, Senator."

They heard Hank blow out a breath, as if he'd been holding it. "All right, I'm convinced."

"Hallelujah," Dylan enthused cryptically. "Now can we get on with this, please?" He didn't wait for a response to his plea. "Where are you?"

Ever since the scene on the courthouse steps, Hank had taken measures to keep ahead of the media hounds. "I've been moving around, trying to stay a step ahead of the press." The silence that met his statement told Hank that Dylan was waiting for him to elaborate. "Staying with different people."

"Your mistresses?" Dylan asked. There was a coldness in his voice.

He didn't expect the answer he heard. "Hell, no," his father hooted. "They're a jealous bunch. They didn't know about each other," he confessed. "Now they're all ready to vivisect me."

"That would save the government the cost of a trial," Dylan commented dryly. He found himself relating to this unreal collection of supermodel blondes. "Can't say I blame them," he said almost under his breath, but still audible enough to be heard. "So exactly where can I meet you?"

"Then you really are serious about wanting to help me?" Hank pressed.

There was a part of Dylan that still couldn't shake the thought that he was going to regret this, but he answered in the affirmative. In a manner of speaking. "Unfortunately, I am."

Hank thought for a moment, then seemed to make up his mind. There were few enough people whom he could trust. Everyone who'd professed friendship and support during the good times had turned on him. The body count was rising as his choices were diminishing.

"Meet me at the house," Hank told him. "I can be there in an hour."

"The house" was his sprawling, incredibly opulent estate in Beverly Hills. There were few like it. There were sheiks who had palaces that might lay claim to rivaling the area that Hank whimsically called home, but there was nothing like it around here. And that was saying a lot, given the affluence that could be found in Beverly Hills.

"Aren't you afraid that the media will ambush you?" Dylan asked. "From what I hear, they're camped out in front of the security gates at the house."

After the scene the other day, Hank wouldn't want to come within fifty yards of the media, but fears had to be faced. "There are ways to get in and out undetected if I have to."

"Is that how you did it?" Dylan wanted to know.

His father obviously wasn't following him. "Did what?"

"Stepped out on Mother all those times that you *were* at home?"

The twenty-room estate, built on the site of a silent-movie great's one-of-a-kind mansion, had incorporated some of that former legend's quirky designs, including an underground passage that ran close to a mile and a quarter, eventually coming out into the basement of the estate next door.

Legend had it that the passage had originally been used by the movie star to sneak away for regular trysts with the woman who eventually became his third wife, when both he and the woman in question were married to other people.

Dylan could almost see his father scowling on the other end of the line.

"This isn't the time for that discussion, Dylan," Hank informed him.

"No, I wouldn't think it would be," Dylan replied glibly. "Okay, one hour," he agreed. "I'll see you there." But then a complicating factor hit him. "But if I go directly to the estate, the newshounds camped outside the estate gates will suspect something is up."

"As long as you don't stop to talk to them, we'll be fine. Knowing and suspecting are two very different things," Hank pointed out.

"You would be the expert on that," Dylan couldn't help observing. "Okay, one hour. I'll be there."

Reaching out, he was about to disconnect the call when he heard his father say, "Oh, and Dylan?"

Now what? "Yes, sir?"

"Thanks." The single word came without a preamble. Not even a mild word of foreshow, a whisper, *something* to give him a clue this was coming.

The one sure thing was that he hadn't expected it. Not from his father. Maybe from one of his father's handlers or from the staff members he was, or had been, running into the ground—*that* he could see.

But from the old man himself? Not possible. And yet, he'd said it. Who knew that the middle of September was the time for miracles?

The single word of gratitude had sounded

genuine. Definitely a first for the old man, Dylan thought cynically.

"Yeah, well, don't go thanking me just yet. We've got a ways to go with this before you're anywhere in the clear."

But Hank was not about to take back what he'd said. "Just knowing you're there, in my corner, means a lot to me, Dylan."

Like you were there in Mother's corner, Dad?

It was on the tip of his tongue to ask that, but it wouldn't serve any purpose, would just stir things up, muddy the waters. The past was the past and his father was not a man who would suddenly have an epiphany because one of his sons had taken him to task for his very tarnished behavior. It just didn't work that way. Not where his father was concerned.

He let the comment go.

"Okay," Dylan repeated, his voice somewhat stilted. "One hour. Security code still the same to get in the gates?" he asked.

"Yes, except that you need to reverse the numbers. I reentered them that way last month."

Dylan wondered if his father even remembered that his son did that unintentionally more times than he liked to think of. Most likely the old man didn't remember that one of his children battled dyslexia.

Nothing new there. Actually remembering how many children he had, would be a major accomplishment for his father.

Legitimate children, Dylan qualified. God only knew how many other women his father had gotten pregnant before this latest one had stepped into the spotlight, demanding her due.

Pressing End, he disconnected the call and shook his head. Though he was accustomed to a fast-paced life, this all still felt like a circus to him. A loon-fest about a man who bore little to no resemblance to the man he'd once known as his father.

Or had thought he'd known, Dylan amended. *Just shows that I wasn't all that bright as a kid,* he thought.

Turning from the desk, he saw that his father's petite guard dog in the smart light-gray suit was watching him. If it didn't seem so incredible, he would have said that there was sympathy in her eyes. But that was impossible; guard dogs didn't feel sympathy. Not that he would have welcomed it anyway.

"He meant that, you know," Cindy told him quietly just as Dylan was about to pick up his hand-stitched leather briefcase and leave.

Which part of the conversation was she referring to? "Meant what?" he asked.

"The part about being grateful to you for offering your help." She had the sense that the senator was feeling rather alone right now, what with his formerly adoring followers suddenly turning on him, recoiling the way people

did when confronted with something danger-
ous and evil.

Dylan shrugged. "Well, like I said, I'm not
doing it for him. He goes down, everyone in
the family's going to be dragged through the
mud with him." He looked at her, wanting no
mistake to be made about this. No false intentions attached to what he was doing. "I'm not
about to see that happen."

She nodded, as if she understood. The smile
on her lips this time around was neither mocking nor cynical. It was, he caught himself
thinking, rather sweet. The next moment, he
pushed the thought aside. The last thing he
needed right now was to be having any sort
of sensual thoughts about one of his father's
women.

"So you're the family crusader?" she was
asking.

He didn't care for labels. Nor did he welcome

any false notions about who or what he was. That was strictly his father's purview.

Shaking his head to negate her assumption, he told her, "I'm just a guy who doesn't want to see his mother and his brothers and sister have to endure any more than they already have."

Feeling suddenly woozy, Cindy leaned her hip against the desk, needing a little support as a vague dizziness threatened to intensify. Her head didn't feel right. Wouldn't that be just perfect, fainting in front of the senator's son?

She struggled to find her way out of the fog. A moment later, much to her relief, the strange dizziness receded. Cindy concentrated, focusing on what Dylan had just said. She wanted to draw attention away from herself.

"And what was it that they—and you—have already endured?"

He shrugged. He wasn't trying to make her think that his family life was unique, just that it was very far from the perfection his father had purported it to be.

"Nothing that a lot of other families of public personalities haven't had to put up with. A husband and father who was never there. Who only took an interest—or pretended to—when it suited his need to appear to be an involved husband and parent."

He shrugged again, but his tone belied this attempt at casualness. "I resented being used," he confessed.

The next moment, Dylan caught himself. What the hell was he doing? Since when did this become true-confessions time? He was usually a great deal better at keeping things to himself. He was gregarious, but schooled in the art of appearing to say much while really saying very little.

Something, he supposed, he'd actually picked up from his father.

"Did you ever stop to think that maybe that

was the only way the senator *could* relate to you and your siblings?" Cindy suggested.

He didn't see how she got from point A to point B. There was an entire river between them. "You mean by using us to pad his résumé, to make himself look like a genuine walking, talking family-values kind of guy?"

He *had* been severely hurt by his father's inattention, Cindy thought. He just wasn't about to admit it to anyone, even himself. Sympathy stirred within her.

"I mean, he had to relate to you within the only realm where he felt comfortable," she said. "The political arena."

He'd concede that she might have a point. "That could be true about us—he never got to know any of us. We were all just little kids when he won his first election and went off to Washington. But what about my mother?" he asked. The answer, as far as he was concerned, was a foregone conclusion. "She knew him before all this political smoke-and-mirrors garbage came in to distract him. If it wasn't for her," he pointed out, "he never would have been able to *become* the U.S. senator from California. It was her money, her inheritance, he used to fund his campaigns."

She was aware of the anger in his eyes and would have backed away, but something he'd said had caught her attention. It didn't add up. He'd said that he and his family had stayed on the home front while his father had gone to Washington. But she'd had the impression that they'd gone with his father.

She asked him about it. "I remember seeing a photograph of the senator with his family with the White House in the background. I got the impression that you weren't playing tourists."

"No, we did live there. For a while. Mother was determined the family would stay together, but the social whirl, the long hours, the constant campaigning—official and covert—got to be too much for her."

He remembered those early years. Remembered wanting to do something to make his mother smile again. Remembered resenting his father for doing this to her. For not giving them a normal life.

"And besides, she hardly saw my father anyway. He was always working late on some committee or other."

Was that when it started, Dad? Did you connect with your first mistresses there, while using that old chestnut on Mother about having to work late? Was it a woman you were "working on" and not a bill?

There was no point in wondering about that, Dylan decided. The time for mending family fences was long gone. He'd meant what he said about doing this just for his mother's sake. If she weren't around, if all this wouldn't take a toll on her pride, he'd let his father twist in the wind, hanging from a rope that the old man had fashioned out of all his failings and short-comings.

The woman with the expressive eyes was still looking at him. Was she expecting some dramatic revelation to be forthcoming? He had already said far more than he should have.

"He really hurt you a great deal, didn't he?" It was in the form of a question, but he sensed that his father's Chief Staff Assistant wasn't asking, she was confirming. He didn't like being backed into a corner, didn't like being deposited into a labeled space. It wasn't the way he operated.

Instead of answering, he picked up his briefcase. "I'm going to take off," he told her. "There's no telling what I'll run into, even just trying to get near the senator's house." He and his siblings had grown up there, but it had never been much of a home to him. More like a museum with a tennis court and sauna.

She nodded, about to turn back to what she'd been doing before he ever walked in. And then she stopped abruptly.

There was absolutely no point in manning the office or getting the senator's files in order, not until she knew whether things were going to change drastically. There was also absolutely no reason to organize files that would ultimately wind up being shredded. Or to draw up schedules that weren't going to be followed.

Looking at the senator's son, she made up her mind quickly. He was probably not going to like this, but she didn't care. She wasn't doing it for him. "I'm going with you."

Chapter 4

The attractive assistant's declaration, coming out of nowhere, took him by surprise. "I don't remember asking you to come along."

The look in her eyes told him she took offense at what he'd just said; the fire in her eyes made her even more attractive. Under different circumstances… But circumstances weren't different and there was no point in going there.

"I don't remember needing permission," she informed him.

Why would she want to come with him? Off the top of his head, he could think of only one reason. "Afraid I'm going to do something to your boss?" He'd nearly said *lover* instead of *boss,* but had caught himself just in time.

Walking out of the senator's office, she led the way to her own, far smaller one, to get her purse before they left. "I just want him to see a friendly face." She looked at him over her shoulder. "Yours obviously isn't."

He had no right to tell her not to come, and if she went with him rather than on her own, he'd get an opportunity to ask her a few more questions about his father. Maybe he'd even get a feeling for just how bad the situation actually was. He had a strong feeling that his father couldn't be trusted to be one-hundred-percent honest with him. Too many years of "embellishing" any questions put to the man had gone by.

He shrugged, negating what had come across as his initial opposition. "Sure, why not? Shall I drive you or do you want to drive me?" he asked her.

Neither of the choices would have been her first. Now inside her office, she crossed to her desk and took her shoulder bag from the bottom drawer. "Why can't we both just drive separately?"

Dylan sized her up for a moment before answering. He was fairly certain he had her number in at least one department: ecology.

"Oh, that's not very green-minded of you. Haven't you heard?" Dylan deadpanned. "Conservation is in, that includes fuel consumption. Going separately would be pretty wasteful."

Though the man sounded sincere as he said it, she instinctively knew he was putting her on. She decided to go along with him for a far more basic reason than taking one car off the road for the space of a round trip; in as much as he'd grown up at the estate and she herself had never been there, Cindy decided it would make more sense and be faster if Dylan were the one to drive.

But, life with her ex had taught her one very important thing—other than not to trust her heart—never take anything for granted. It was always best to have things spelled out before-hand.

She glanced into the oversize purse to make sure she had everything, then slipped it onto her shoulder. "If you drive me, how will I get back here once you're finished talking to the senator?"

Cindy Jensen struck him as an intelligent woman, he thought, so the fact that she didn't just assume what he was about to tell her made him wonder about the kind of people she was used to dealing with. Did they just run out on her whenever the whim hit?

"I'll drive you back," he told her cheerfully. "Why? Did you think I'd leave you stranded? I'm not that kind of a guy," he assured her.

She was going to have to trust him. Besides, she reasoned, she could always call a cab.

"Frankly, I have no idea what kind of a guy you are, Mr. Kelley," she informed him coolly.

"One who likes to be called Dylan instead of Mr. Kelley," he told her. "As for not knowing the kind of person I am, while we're going to the estate, I'll do my best to fill you in. Go ahead," he urged as they walked out of the suite of offices housed within a much larger shell, "ask me anything."

Out in the hallway, Dylan started to lead the way to the elevators. He was surprised when his father's assistant caught hold of his arm, halting him in mid stride. When he looked at her quizzically, she wasn't moving.

"Not that way," she told him, indicating the elevator with a nod of her head. "The reporters are all over the ground floor by now, waiting to pounce on anyone remotely attached to the senator. No telling when we'd be free of them if they waylay us coming out of the elevator. We'll take the back stairs."

Turning on his heel, he followed her toward the stairwell. "And no one will be waiting to ambush us there?" he asked skeptically.

She knew it sounded rather strange. "You'd be surprised at how simplistic and tunnel-visioned these reporters can be. They assume the people they're tracking are lazy and incapable of eluding someone of their intellectual caliber."

A flicker of admiration passed over his face. Dylan held the stairwell door open for her. "You've done this before."

She supposed her smile was a tad smug. "Once or twice."

"For my father?" he asked. Dylan couldn't remember there being an occasion for a media feeding frenzy of this magnitude before. Until now, the old man had led a charmed life. There might have been vague rumors every now and then, but nothing serious had ever stuck.

Cindy debated just ignoring his question,

then decided that there was no reason to hide anything. "I started out working for Josh Sawyer."

"The actor?" When she nodded in response, he had to admit he was somewhat impressed. And curious. "Why did you switch jobs?"

She saw no point in mentioning Dean, or his ever-growing jealous streak and the marks it eventually began to leave on her. Or that, if it hadn't been for the fact that Dean liked having money so much, he would have kept her barefoot and housebound.

God, what an idiot she'd been ever to have thought she actually loved that man. Dean didn't know the meaning of the word. The sentiment was completely wasted on him.

"The senator needed someone to fill a vacancy on his staff and Josh Sawyer had suddenly decided to change his home base. He wanted to be seen as an international celebrity, so he was going to move abroad. That had no allure for me," she said, raising her voice ever so slightly in order to be heard above the click of her heels on the metal stairs. "Me, I like being in the United States."

He could easily understand that. What he couldn't understand was why someone of her intelligence could remain working for his father like some lackey with a sixth-grade education. Unless, of course, it was because of the obvious reason—that his father's power and position, not to mention his eternal gift of gab, had seduced her.

And kept on seducing her.

It wasn't something he wanted to dwell on for the time being.

Once out of the stairwell, Dylan led the way through the parking structure until he reached his car. The vehicle was parked on the far side of the very first level.

Pressing a button on his key ring, he unlocked the vehicle when they were still several yards away. All four locks popped to attention.

He crossed to the passenger side and held the door open for her. "Why do you stay with him?" he wanted to know. She'd made him really curious. He just couldn't picture his father and the young woman in the same conversation, much less locked in a clinch, panting and sweaty in bed.

He had manners, Cindy thought. He held her door open as she got into the vehicle. Unusual for someone who seemed to come on so brashly. She waited until she buckled up before answering him.

"Because I believe in what the senator stands for. Because he's passionate."

Getting in on the driver's side, Dylan looked at her. "Yeah, I'll just bet."

Her resentment flared instantly. He'd just convicted her of a crime without so much as doing her the courtesy of questioning her.

Whatever had happened to innocent until proven guilty? Was that just a platitude, or was that something reserved for people this annoying man actually liked?

"I mean about his political principles," she informed Dylan coolly.

Her eyes narrowed. Maybe she should tell him that she'd changed her mind about coming with him. Maybe this was the perfect opportunity to get out. The thought of being trapped in his car, enduring his thinly veiled contempt, held absolutely no appeal to her.

Her regard appeared to Dylan to be less than friendly as she said, "I don't think I like what you're implying."

Okay, maybe he had been out of line, but he had a feeling that he probably hadn't. To be fair, he gave her the opportunity to convince him. His eyes all but penetrated her skin, going clear down to the spine. Only then, acting as a human lie detector, did he continue talking.

"You're telling me that you weren't involved with my father."

"Of course I was—and am—involved with your father. I work for the man. I *have* been working for him for the last two years. I'm 'involved' in every aspect of the senator's political life."

That wasn't what he meant and she knew it. Since she seemed determined to play this game of semantics, he gave it one more try. "And what about his private one? Are you involved in that as well?"

He didn't let up, did he? Well, she wasn't about to admit to something that wasn't true, no matter how many ways he framed his question.

Cindy gave him a look that would have frozen hell over, then said, "I don't have to dignify that with an answer—but I will." For what had to be the fourth time, she repeated her official title. "I am the senator's Chief Staff Assistant. I coordinate his meetings, take care of his flight arrangements. Make sure he gets to his meetings and interviews on time and is prepared. That means making sure he has his speeches with him and is apprised of everything he needs to know for whatever the occasion, be it a press conference or the opening of a new supermarket. But when the senator goes home for the night and closes his door, my job ends." Running out of breath, she said, "Am I making myself clear?" She'd pretty much had just about enough of this.

Dylan's mouth curved. He caught himself liking her spirit—and really hoping she was telling him the truth. Because that made things a lot less complicated.

He nodded his head. "Very."

She couldn't tell if he actually believed her or had just stepped back to keep from turning this into an argument. Nothing in his tone gave her any indication of what he was thinking—or feeling.

She took a guess. "You don't believe me."

While he would have liked to believe that she was as innocent as she pretended to be, Dylan couldn't quite get himself to buy what she'd just told him. Not in light of what he knew about his father. The man had a wandering eye, and, in his place, Dylan knew that he damn well wouldn't go shopping for meals in another city when he could have a home-cooked one right here, courtesy of his rather sexy, intriguing staff assistant.

He answered her honestly. He had no interest in playing games. "I don't see how, given the way you look, my father could keep his hands off you."

The blunt statement took her breath away for a moment. Cindy was torn between feeling flattered and being insulted.

Six of one, half a dozen of the other, she

thought, deciding to take the middle ground. She took his assessment of her looks as a compliment, but was insulted by what he seemed to think of her morals. He had no idea about her marital status, but it was a known fact that his father was married. What kind of a woman would she be, having an affair with a married man?

The senator's less-than-endearing son needed to be educated about some basic points, and she might as well be the one to do it, especially since there appeared to be no one else available for the job.

"Number one—the senator is not the rutting pig that everyone seems to think he is. I've never walked in on him in a compromising position, never had any occasion to suspect that he was engaged in anything immoral—until this story broke." And, she had to admit, the evidence was pretty damning, but she was going to reserve judgment until she had more proof one way or another. "And number two— what makes you think I'm such a pushover that all he has to do is crook his finger and I'd jump into his bed? My morals, I'll have you know, are completely intact, thank you very much. I don't jump into anyone's bed, least of all the senator's."

"Good for you." Why did the image of her leaping into a bed seem so damn appealing? And so vivid? "And to answer your question as to why I'd think you'd 'jump' into his bed, it's because my father is pretty damn charismatic. The man could charm the fur off a fox if he set his mind to it."

She raised her chin slightly. Defiantly. "Lucky for me I'm not a fox."

That same fire in her eyes made her seem even more compelling and attractive than she already was. The old-fashioned description "spitfire" flashed through his mind out of no-where. That was an apt, succinct description of her, he thought. Once again he regretted that they'd met under these circumstances.

But then, if it hadn't been for these circumstances, there would have been no reason for him to have anything to do with his father's world and he wouldn't have met her anyway.

He thought of what she'd just said about not being a fox. "I'd say that's lucky for both of us."

She looked at him in amused disbelief. Was he coming on to her? Or had all this talk about whether she was part of the senator's love life made her irrationally sensitive, anticipating things that weren't about to happen?

"Do women usually respond to that line?" she asked him.

It hadn't been a line, it had been the first thing that came into his head because he was happy that she wasn't one of his father's little playmates. That she was better than that, smarter than that.

What did it matter what she was? a voice in his head asked. He didn't attempt to fashion an answer.

"I wouldn't know," he replied, looking back at the road. "I don't use lines."

He could have sworn he *heard* her smile.

L.A. traffic, never good, was relatively decent around this time, at least today, and they made it to his father's Beverly Hills estate within the hour, as promised.

Just as he'd anticipated, the immediate area before the tall, imposing gates was filled to bursting with parked news vans and milling-about, restless reporters.

He felt the woman beside him stiffen as they came closer to the scene.

It was obvious from her reaction that she hadn't anticipated this much of a crowd. "Omigod," she murmured in stunned disbelief.

The smile on his lips had no mirth behind it. "A little staggering, isn't it?"

"Don't these people have anything better to do?" It was a rhetorical question, brimming with anger that had yet to spill out.

While she was angry at the senator for doing this to himself, to his family, and for disappointing her, she was even angrier at the media for turning him into prey, reducing him to hiding and sneaking around like a common criminal.

"Apparently not," Dylan answered. "It appears that my illustrious father is the story of the hour. Most likely of the week and maybe even of the month as well. The media likes to squeeze a story dry, holding it up to the light, examining it from every possible angle and getting everything they can out of it before tossing it aside, a shell of what it once was as they move on."

His hands tightened on the steering wheel as he drove by, neither speeding up nor slowing down, determined not to do anything to draw their attention to him. There were so many different reporters from so many different venues, he gave up trying to do a head count.

"All we can hope for," he told Cindy, "is that some bigger, juicier scandal crops up on the horizon sooner rather than later."

He heard her sigh in response. Glancing in her direction, he saw her shaking her head. The look on her face was one of a deep, pervading sadness. She really appeared to be upset by all this, he thought. He concluded that her soul hadn't been jaded yet. He wondered how long it would be before it was.

"You didn't have to come," he pointed out as he continued driving, past the estate's entrance.

"Yes, I did," she insisted with feeling. "In the face of all this, it's obvious he needs to feel that someone's on his side. Besides you," she added, not wanting to insult him. He didn't, after all, have to be here no matter how much he protested.

"I'm not on his side," Dylan reminded her. "I just want to get this resolved with as little bloodletting as possible and move on."

"Speaking of moving, exactly where are you going?" she asked him. "The mansion," turning her head, she nodded toward it, "is back there."

"Yes, I know," he answered, unfazed. "A mile down the road is Dr. Richard McCallum's house. Actually, it's more like a palace, but for the purposes of narrative, I'll call it a house—"

Impatient, she wanted him to get to the point. "You can call it Edgar if you want," she said tersely. "What does it have to do with my question?"

"I'm getting to that," he said, deliberately enunciating every word.

He had no idea why, but he got a kick out of sparring with her. He supposed it was the adult equivalent of pulling her pigtails and running.

The exasperated look she gave him said he

was playing on her last nerve. Dylan sped up his answer. "There's a passageway that runs between the good doctor's house and the evil senator's house," he told her whimsically. "I'm going there so that we can go back to my father's place without having to fight our way through a wall of reporters."

She looked at him a little uncertainly. "And you're sure about this secret passageway?"

"I'm sure. As kids, my brothers and I used to pretend we were pirates. We'd bury our 'treasure' in the doctor's garden by coming from ours and using the secret passageway. Of course, that meant we had to let the doctor's annoyingly gawky daughter play with us, but it was a small price to pay for feeding our fantasies."

That sounded like a colorful—and satisfying—childhood to her. "Well, you don't seem to have suffered too much as the senator's son."

"I didn't," he agreed. "Until I was old enough

to understand that most kids had fathers who did more than pose for pictures with them before taking off for weeks, sometimes months, at a time."

They were on the doctor's property now. Within a couple of minutes, Dylan was pulling the car up before a towering structure that actually did resemble a medieval castle, right down to the stones artfully placed one on top of another to give it a genuine appearance.

Getting out, he waved at someone within "the palace" before coming around to her side of the vehicle. Not standing on ceremony, Cindy had already gotten out.

Squinting, she tried to make out who Dylan had just waved at. She didn't see anyone. "Waving at the doctor's daughter?" she guessed, amused.

"At his butler." She looked at him in surprise. "Spooky guy seems to have no life beyond standing in the foyer, watching the air move and, on occasion, opening the door. For this, I hear, he's paid rather well. It feeds the doctor's own fantasies," he explained. "Not everyone can afford to have a British butler opening their front door for them."

Cindy was beginning to think that Dylan Kelley had had a very strange upbringing after all.

He barely rang the doorbell—which sounded like the chimes at Westminster Abbey—before the massive doors opened.

A tall, gaunt, balding, almost anemic-looking older man stood in the space. He was dressed in black livery. The white shirt was a stark contrast, bringing her attention to his pallor. He had an incredibly pale complexion that a vampire would have envied.

"Hello, Wakefield. I'll need to make use of the passageway."

The butler didn't look surprised or ruffled.

Instead, he nodded as if this were an everyday request rather than a rare event.

"Of course, Master Cole," he said through thin, bloodless lips that appeared to be barely moving. "You know where it is."

Not bothering to correct the man, Dylan just nodded and went on his way. "I do. And thanks."

Cindy realized he had her by the hand and was towing her behind him. When had he taken her hand? Moreover, why had the old butler called him by a wrong name?

Deliberately removing her hand from his, Cindy said, "He called you Cole. Why would he do that?"

"Because I have a twin brother named Cole."

A twin brother. What else was going to pop out at her?

It was, Cindy thought, hurrying to keep up

with Dylan and his extra-long legs, a little like Alice falling down the rabbit's hole. Except that she felt as if she was still in free fall.

Chapter 5

Dylan had remembered to take the thin pencil flashlight from his glove compartment with him. He used it now to illuminate the passageway that ran between Dr. McCallum's mansion and the one his parents owned, walking a step ahead of his father's assistant.

Following him, Cindy was careful not to let Dylan get more than a couple of steps away from her. She'd never been all that crazy about the dark and trying to find her way in the blackened underground was just about the worst of all possible scenarios as far as she was concerned.

It felt as if they had been walking for a while now. Was there only one path, or was it possible to get lost? "How far apart did you say the houses were?"

He knew what she was getting at. His sister Lana had been exceedingly uncomfortable in the dark as a kid. She'd had the same look on her face when they were down here as Cindy now had.

"Not as far as they seem in the dark," he told her. "Don't worry. There're no bats around here. As far as I know," he qualified

He'd done that on purpose, Cindy thought. Still, she looked around her nervously. Bats slept during the daytime, didn't they? "You had to put it that way, didn't you?"

He laughed, then forced himself to look more serious. "Actually, yes. I get to have so little fun as a defense attorney." He added just the proper amount of mournfulness to his tone.

Taking his hand with the flashlight in it, she

deliberately pointed it upward. Nothing. Cindy felt somewhat better and released his hand. She ignored his amused expression.

"If fun was your goal, you picked the wrong career," she pointed out, pretending, for a moment, that they were actually having a serious conversation on the subject.

"I guess I did."

Walking a little further, he turned again to see if she was keeping up—just in time to see her stumble and trip over something on the ground. Reacting automatically, he caught her before she could hit the ground, his arms quickly closing around her in order to keep her upright.

Cindy lost her breath. Not because she'd almost tripped, but because Dylan's arms had closed around her, pulling her close and imprisoning her against his chest. The firmness of his torso registered with her brain, the favorable reaction it created instantly at odds with her automatic one: stiffening as if in anticipation of a blow.

She tried to talk herself into relaxing—on both counts. This wasn't Dean. She wasn't about to get manhandled.

It also became obvious to her that this was not a man who threw back beers and munched chips in his off hours. A gym, or at least exercise equipment, was apparently woven into the attorney's everyday world. You didn't get a body that hard by slacking off or ordering it from a catalog. It took diligent work and discipline, qualities she had always admired.

It put her on less than solid ground here.

"You okay?" he asked, slowly regulating his own breathing so that she wouldn't notice she'd all but knocked the air out of him. He peered down into her face, searching for an answer before she could say anything. He'd felt her stiffen far more than the situation warranted. What was that all about?

"Yes." Cindy practically bit off the one-word retort, embarrassed more than she was willing to admit, even to herself.

His hands still on either side of her torso, as if to told her steady, he glanced down at the ground. "What did you trip over?" He'd wanted to ask her why she'd stiffened the way she had as well, but had a feeling that she wouldn't welcome that question—or give him an answer.

Was that her heart hammering like that? *Why?* Cindy demanded silently, impatiently. She hadn't fallen, he'd caught her in time.

Maybe, she thought, she would have been better off if she'd just fallen down. Embarrassed, but ultimately better off.

"How should I know?" It took effort not to snap at him. He made her nervous standing this close to her. For more than one reason. "I can't see anything."

Dylan glanced down again. "Then you shouldn't have worn high heels," he pointed out.

Unless she was home, barefoot, she *always* wore high heels. It was just part of who she was. "When I got dressed this morning, I wasn't planning on hiking in the bowels of the earth."

She saw his mouth curve, could almost *feel* the smile on his lips. "You should always be prepared for the unexpected."

The unexpected, in this case, wasn't whatever she'd tripped over, it was the flash of warmth she'd felt just before her body had gone rigid when Dylan's arms had closed around her.

Taking a breath, Cindy tried to step back, away from him. It would have been far easier to do if the man had already let go of her. But his hands were still resting on either side of her waist, just above her hips and she could *swear* she felt her body temperature rising a few degrees more.

That's not what you're about these days, remember? It's not just you anymore, a haunting voice reminded her. The same inner voice that seemed to infiltrate her days and her nights these last few months, reminding her she was no longer alone.

"You can let go of me now," she told him. "I'm not falling anymore."

She thought she saw a gleam enter his eyes, but the light was exceedingly limited so she could have been wrong.

"You're sure?" he asked, his voice almost teasing her.

"I'm sure."

"All right, then." Dylan dropped his hands from her sides. He couldn't help noticing how delicate she felt, in direct contrast to the image of a tough little go-getter she was attempting to present. He also couldn't help noticing that for a second there, she'd stiffened as if a wave of fear had passed over her. "Let's go find my illustrious father."

"You know," she said as they resumed making their way through the tunnel, "you might want to think about dropping that very large chip from your shoulder when you see him."

If he had a chip—which, Dylan was sure he didn't—he'd earned the right to it. His father hadn't even tried to get involved in their lives, had never reached out to any of them, with the exception of Lana. Lana was the only one of them who, time and again, stood up for their father; and in those rare instances when his father had a spare moment to spend with the family, he spent it with Lana. She was the baby of the family and he doted on her as much as he was capable of doting on anyone.

"*I'm* not the one who needs *him*," Dylan emphasized. "He's the one who needs decent legal representation—and help," he added.

The single word encompassed far more than just the need for counsel. Senator Hank Kelley needed a friend, someone who could get between him and the media, to act, quite frankly, as a shield. Given that, Dylan was beginning to think that perhaps he should rethink his role in all this. How far was he willing to go to help a man he was struggling not to loathe?

"All very true," she willingly agreed. Cindy squinted, trying to see if there was any sign of journey's end yet. This roundabout route might be necessary to avoid the press in front of the senator's mansion, but it still gave her the creeps. "But no one likes having their nose rubbed in it—or to be made to feel like someone's outcast poor relation. The senator," she reminded him, "is a proud man."

He laughed shortly. "He's also a deluded man, because from where I'm standing, he's got nothing to be proud of."

Cindy took umbrage on the senator's behalf.

The man's record in the Senate was the reason she hadn't jumped ship at the first hint of this storm breaking over them.

"Would you like me to go over the bills the senator either initiated or backed, bills that helped to dig the people of this state out of the deep, deep hole they found themselves in?"

Dylan held up one hand as if to physically block the very idea. "Spare me," he said.

Cindy stopped walking, anger gathering in her eyes. "No, I don't think I should." Surprised at her combative tone, Dylan turned around to look at her. "Look," she said, "if you're going to offer him a hand, offer him a hand. Don't thumb your nose at him with the other one. Or are you just doing this so you don't have a guilty conscience?"

He didn't follow how she'd arrived at that conclusion. "How's that again?"

"The way I see it," she explained, "if you 'offer' your father help and he turns you down because of your offensive attitude, well, you can soothe your conscience by telling yourself you tried. That way, down the line, it's not your fault if the senator gets torn apart in the public arena. Not your fault that every good thing he's ever done is forgotten in the light of the fact that he has a runaway libido and supposedly dipped into campaign funds to shower his mistresses with gifts and provide them with affluent lifestyles."

The passageway looked as if it hadn't been used in years, not since he and his brothers and sister had played here. Except that, of course, his father must have just used this—if he was at the mansion.

The heaviness of the dust-laden air was oppressive, Dylan thought, wiping the back of his wrist across the perspiration along his forehead.

"I take it by your tone that you don't believe he did."

She believed that he did—and that he didn't. It depended on what part Dylan was referring to. "While I believe, unfortunately, that the senator did get sidetracked by more than one willing political groupie—" a group she had absolutely no use for and strongly disliked "—I know him. He's not an idiot. He wouldn't risk everything, throw everything away just because he was trying to impress one of his so-called mistresses. He didn't take any campaign funds."

Dylan saw it differently. "He wouldn't be the first man to be brought down by a woman— or by rampant lust." He smiled to himself, unaware that she had caught a glimpse of his expression. "Men don't always think with their brains."

"Men don't always think," she corrected. "You could have stopped there," she told him. "And I'm not arguing that. I'm arguing that the senator wouldn't throw everything away—or think he was bulletproof. He's not a fool," she concluded with feeling.

Again, they were on opposite sides of this point of view. "Every man's a fool if the right woman's involved. Or wrong woman as the case may be," Dylan amended with a shrug.

They'd finally come to a door and, Cindy sincerely hoped, the end of their unusual journey. She turned from the door and looked at him, vaguely curious. "Are you speaking from experience?"

If she was looking to box him in, he neatly sidestepped the effort. So far, no woman had made a fool of him and he intended to keep it that way.

"I'm speaking as a lawyer who's seen a lot of strange behavior on the part of seemingly intelligent adults—male and female," he added.

She wondered if that was all it was. Cindy pressed her lips together, debating whether or not to push the point, then decided to retreat—

in a way. For the senator's sake, she couldn't risk really antagonizing his son.

"Well, please just treat him with respect," she requested.

The easy thing would have just been to say "yes," but Dylan stubbornly refused to concede the point. For some reason, whether or not he ever saw this woman again, he wanted her to understand where he was coming from. "He surrendered his right to that a long time ago."

Okay, she'd approach it from another angle. Because, when he spoke to his father, if his attitude came through, she knew the senator—the man would issue his son his walking papers.

"Be that as it may, be the bigger man," she told him. "Pretend you're prepared to believe his side of the story. Who knows?" she said a tad too brightly. "It just might be true."

The intended sarcasm was not missed by Dylan.

While they'd been talking, they'd gone through the connecting door on the other side of the passageway, then up the basement stairs. Inside the family estate now, Dylan stopped for a moment and looked around. The last time he'd been here was when? A couple of years ago? More? He wasn't sure about the year, but he remembered the day. His mother had thrown a Christmas party and they had all tried to come together from the various places they'd scattered to as their lives unfolded before them.

Cole lived in Montana these days, running the ranch that the two of them bought from their grandmother. Lana was studying in Europe. At the moment, she was in Paris, but from what he'd heard, she was going to be heading back to Florence, where she was studying that city's rich art history.

The rest of the family was definitely closer than Lana, but no easier to pin down, really. Or any more readily coaxed into returning for an audience with their mother, who had grown more and more introverted over the years. Something else Dylan had blamed on his father.

Excuses abounded from his siblings, but then Christmas wound up making everyone a little more accommodating. Added to that, Sarah Kelley had promised that their father would be there to celebrate the season as well. She hadn't yet learned not to make promises she had no control over keeping.

But she'd learned that afternoon. His father sent a huge bouquet of long-stemmed roses and a card from the florist, expressing his regrets about not being there, but "something pressing" had come up.

Undoubtedly, Dylan thought cynically, his father was the one doing the pressing and there was a warm, willing, nubile recipient on the receiving end.

He wasn't moving, Cindy realized. "Something wrong?" she asked, once her eyes were accustomed to the light again.

There was no point in talking about his father's no-show. It was just one incident among many. Instead, Dylan just shrugged away the question. "Just thinking how the more things change, the more they remain the same."

That was definitely not going to make anyone's news bulletin, she thought. "Given to profound thoughts as well, I see. Maybe you should have that embroidered on a towel."

He raised a dark, almost perfectly shaped eyebrow as he regarded her more closely. "Someone wake up on the wrong side of the crypt this morning?" Dylan wanted to know.

She supposed she *was* a little testy, but he certainly didn't help her mood. "I don't like having everything upset like this—me included," she tagged on.

If worse came to worst, his father's Chief Staff Assistant would just move on, Dylan thought. He had no doubt that she could bounce back quickly. She looked resilient enough to be able to do that.

"I'm sure you can find work somewhere else—" he began.

Cindy was quick to cut him off. He had to be made to understand something. "This isn't about a paycheck, Mr. Kelley, it's about dedication. It's about believing in something."

Instead of answering her, Dylan had stopped short, looking over her head. She knew instantly that there was someone behind her. Cindy turned around to see an older, solidly built woman, dressed in somber, conservative shades of gray. There was a hint of a welcoming smile on her lined face.

"Hello, Mr. Dylan. You're looking well."

"So are you, Martha," he told the house-keeper warmly. "Is he here?" It was understood who "he" was. There was no need to elaborate.

"Yes, he just got here a few minutes ago." She nodded at the door behind him, the one that led to the passageway. "He told me to be expecting you." Her eyes shifted over to Cindy. "He didn't say you'd be bringing a friend."

Cindy bristled at being so cavalierly dismissed. She'd struggled most of her life to be taken seriously. "I'm the senator's Chief Staff Assistant. Cindy Jensen," she told the woman, introducing herself.

"You know," Dylan said, leaning down to gain Cindy's ear, "you really should think about having that printed up on a card and just handing it out every time you're tempted to refer to your credentials."

Cindy couldn't get a handle on him. Was he just irreverent? Or was he actually severely jaded? Perhaps a cynic? Or was he, beneath all that, a son who had been hurt by a father's continual inattention?

She supposed he might be a combination of all of the above. But Dylan Kelley, malcontent son, wasn't her concern, she reminded herself. The senator was.

"Right this way," Martha was saying, turning on the heel of her very sensible shoe. With a beckoning gesture, she led the way out of the foyer.

Dylan draped an arm across the woman's broad back. "You're looking younger than ever, Martha," he commented.

"And you still haven't learned how to lie smoothly, my boy." The woman was fairly beaming. "But I appreciate the effort," she assured him fondly.

In the hallway, Martha stopped before a closed door. They could feel music throbbing through the door into the hallway. She gestured them toward the room, a shepherd herding her sheep. "He's in the library. Go easy on him," she advised Dylan quietly.

Dylan glanced at Cindy before responding. "You're not the first to say that."

What was it about his father that brought out this protective streak in women? Women who might be expected to react indignantly to his behavior? *Alleged* behavior, the lawyer in him felt he needed to qualify. But alleged or not, why women felt compelled to champion his father was a mystery to him.

When he walked into the room, the senator's back was to him, but he could see what his father was holding in his hand. The glass was half-empty. He was willing to bet it hadn't been that way a few minutes ago.

"A little early in the day to be drinking, isn't it, Dad?" Dylan asked, not bothering to hide the coolness in his voice.

Thinking himself alone, Hank was surprised

to hear his son's voice and swung around. Lost in his dark thoughts, he hadn't heard the door open or anyone come in. He shrugged in response to Dylan's rhetorical question and regarded the chunky glass in his hand for a moment.

"Not if you've been up around the clock. For me, it's actually the tail end of one hell of an endless day." He became aware of Cindy's presence and for a split second, looked embarrassed. "Why did you bring her?" he asked gruffly.

"He didn't bring me," Cindy said, stepping forward. She looked at him, at his apparently less-than-controlled state and told him, "*I* brought me. I thought you might need my support."

Hank's mouth quirked in what might have passed as a self-deprecating smile. "What I need at this point," he informed her, doing his best to sound philosophical, "is a miracle." His face softened just a little. "Got one of those in your pocket, Cindy?"

Her smile went beyond that of an employee for her boss. It was that of a loving daughter, grieving for her father's fall from grace. "Must have left it in my other skirt."

"Maybe next time," he replied.

Taking another swig, Hank sighed deeply, as if there was just no way for him ever really to catch his breath again. Never to find a way out of the quagmire he'd found himself in. Certainly never a way to make things right again. The gravity of the situation—and the slow awareness that he wasn't going to be able to talk or charm his way out of it—was beginning to really sink in. And it was taking its toll on him.

He was too old to start over again, he thought. And right now, too damn tired as well. He'd never thought that any of his matrimonial missteps would come back to haunt him. And certainly not in spades, the way they had these last few days.

Floundering, needing help to find his way, Hank looked at his son. His successful son, he couldn't help adding. "So, what do we do, Dylan?" he asked. "Do you see a way out of this for me?"

"Have you thought of falling on your sword?" Dylan asked, his voice devoid of any telltale emotion.

"Dylan!" Cindy cried, stunned and angry.

"Actually," the senator admitted, looking into the bottom of his glass as if the answers might be there, "yes, I have. But I'm afraid I'm not that heroic. I need a solution that's a little less drastic. A little less bloody."

"The first step," Dylan said evenly, as if laying out the strategy to win the next football game, "is to stop feeling sorry for yourself.

You're not the victim here," he reminded his father.

The smile on his face was fashioned out of irony. "Funny, I thought I was."

Dylan moved his head from side to side, negating what his father had just said. "The victim is Mother," Dylan pointed out. "And everyone who ever made the mistake of believing in you."

Cindy swung around to look at the senator's son. What was he doing—tearing his father down and then stomping on the pieces? He was supposed to be helping the senator, not destroying what little confidence and hope he might have left. Her temper flared.

"Dylan—"

But Hank waved her into silence. "No, he's right." Still holding the glass in his hands, Hank sank down on the sofa, feeling defeat in every tissue in his body. "He's right," he repeated.

The problem was, Hank thought, draining what was left in his glass, his son didn't realize just how right he actually was.

Chapter 6

"Still," Hank went on to admit in what was a completely unguarded moment, allowing a deep sigh to escape and showing—at least to Cindy, whose heart went out to him—the depths of his vulnerability, "when I came home just now, I was hoping that I'd find your mother waiting for me. But Martha told me that she'd packed up and left the day the story broke."

Dylan stared at his father, stunned. Was the man seriously deluded? Or was his father far too self-centered to understand what he'd done to his wife? To his family? Until this moment, he'd thought of his father as an intelligent man.

Now, he wasn't so sure.

"Really? Dylan asked incredulously. "You really expected her to be here, waiting for you?"

"Really," his father replied with more than a little conviction. Granted, Dylan thought, his mother had certainly never flagged in her support of his father. Of course, there hadn't been any reporters hounding her because there hadn't been any scandal to contend with at the time. "According to the vows," the senator was saying, "your mother was supposed to stand by me no matter what transpired."

No doubt about it, the man really *was* deluded, Dylan decided. "Forgive me," he said coolly, "but the quote is 'in sickness and in health. For richer or poorer.' I don't recall *ever* hearing anything about hanging around while a spouse commits serial adultery."

A self-deprecating smile played on Hank's lips. He hadn't had a hand in it, but at least Sarah had raised a son they could both be proud of. One whose head was on straight and who wasn't intimidated or given to pandering because he hoped to get something out of it. The people he'd worked with—with the lone exception of the young woman standing beside his son—all "yessed" him to death to his face and, he had no doubt, plotted against him behind his back. They'd all run like mice from a sinking ship the moment this story broke.

"I suppose I deserve that," Hank allowed with a resigned nod of his head.

That and so much more, Dylan thought. But all he said in response was, "You have any doubts that you do?"

Hank laughed shortly. *Isn't going to give an inch, this one, is he?* "No, I guess not."

All right, she'd held her tongue long enough, Cindy thought angrily. Yes, the senator had behaved badly, *very* badly. But they were here to figure out how to move forward, not how to flog a man who was clearly down.

"Rehashing this," Cindy informed Dylan crisply, "isn't going to help anything. Now if you're here to help mount a defense for the senator, let's start mounting it. If not, maybe you should leave."

There was fire in her eyes, Dylan noted, fascinated despite himself. How had his father merited such loyalty from her? Again, he couldn't help wondering the extent of their relationship. *Did* it go beyond the office? And how deeply? She didn't strike him as someone who would be willing to take second place to a squadron of mistresses, or as a woman who would be a home wrecker, but then, he hadn't known her even for the length of a day, so maybe his gut was wrong.

"I can't leave," he reminded her, trying to play it light. "At least, not without you. I'm your ride, remember?"

He watched as those same fiery eyes narrowed now, their laser beams focused solely on him.

She was not about to allow this man to spend even a split second thinking he could manipulate her in any manner, shape or form. Those days, thanks to the senator, were behind her.

"Don't worry, Mr. Kelley, I'm not without resources. I assure you that I can get back to the office without you." Turning toward Senator Kelley, she said, "If you point me in the right direction, I'll see about making you a cup of coffee." She glanced down at his empty glass on the coffee table and tactfully amended, "A *strong* cup of coffee."

"I can show you where it is," Dylan offered. Without waiting for her to turn him down, he began to cross toward the threshold. "Coming?" he asked, looked at Cindy over his shoulder.

Cindy looked somewhat reluctant, then fell into place beside him. "Coming," she echoed.

Dylan led the way through the opulent maze he and his siblings had once played explorer in. It was hard to think that he had once been innocent enough to do that. It made him almost nostalgic.

He looked at the woman at his side, curiosity stirring despite his efforts to put a lid on it. "I thought assistants didn't do things like get coffee or tea anymore."

"Because it's demeaning?" she guessed.

Dylan inclined his head as he guided her through what his mother had called the family dining room, as opposed to the formal one where important people gathered and were entertained—people who had gotten his father elected as a senator in the first place.

"Something like that," he told his father's feisty assistant.

Cindy shook her head, as if amused that he subscribed to something so stereotypical. "Assistants do what they need to do in order to assist," she told him pointedly, adding, "Besides, I'm finally comfortable enough in my own skin not to be threatened by something so insignificant as bringing the senator a cup of coffee when he clearly needs one."

Dylan had caught one important word and had barely heard the rest of her statement. *"Finally?"* he repeated, intrigued that she should use this particular word. She already struck him as someone who didn't bandy words about haphazardly. She used them more like precise tools. So why *finally?*

"Finally," Cindy affirmed, leaving the word standing on its own.

Okay, that had to mean something, didn't it? His curiosity grew, multiplying drastically. He studied her face. No secrets were being given away there. It was shut down, tight as a fortress.

"You're not going to elaborate, are you?" It wasn't a guess.

Only then did the hint of a satisfied smile—at his expense, no doubt, he thought—surface.

"No, I'm not," she told him. Senator's son or not, he had no business poking into her life. It had no bearing on the senator's present problem and that was all Dylan Kelley needed to know.

Ultimately he and the senator's Chief Staff Assistant remained at the estate for a little more than an hour. During that time, he plied his father with questions about his dealings with other women as well as what, if anything, he'd been doing with any left-over campaign funds.

When it came to the mistresses, Dylan felt he needed to know exactly how many there were, their names and whatever his father could remember about each, whether or not he thought the information was important.

"Why?" his father had asked. He was unaccustomed to being grilled so closely and this true-confessions session was clearly taking a toll on him. Even a passing stranger could see that he desperately wanted to leave the whole mess far behind him. Buried if possible.

The *why* should have been apparent to him, Dylan thought. "So I can ascertain how much of a liability each is to us, both on the stand and in the general scheme of things."

His father seemed to take heart in the pronoun his son had used and grudgingly conceded that he had a point, at which time he proceeded to give as much information as he could. In some cases, because the women were apparently such casual acquaintances, there wasn't much.

The word *mistress,* he assured his son, was far too liberally bandied about. Most of the time, it wasn't even applicable. One or two liaisons in a motel did not instantly transform a woman into a mistress.

Finally, because he had several loose ends to take care of before he could officially begin the leave of absence he'd gotten from his firm, Dylan called an end to this first meeting.

Cindy observed that it was hard to say which of the two men looked more relieved to see it end—the senator or his son.

Gathering his things together, Dylan promised to be in touch very soon and with that he walked out of the room. He hadn't bothered to shake his father's hand. The senator, Cindy noted, looked a little upset, but said nothing. Instead, he looked in her direction. A weak smile creased his lips. "Thanks for coming," he said to her.

Her heart ached for the man, even if he had brought this all on himself. "It's going to be all right," she promised him, giving him a quick hug before hurrying after the departing Dylan.

Kelley's legs were far too long, she thought, annoyed as she lengthened her own stride to catch up. "Just because I don't mind serving the senator coffee doesn't mean I automatically walk five paces behind you," she called after Dylan, raising her voice so he could hear her.

Dylan immediately slowed down just as they reached the beginning of the passageway. "Sorry, I was just thinking."

"About bailing?" she guessed, glancing at his expression.

He wouldn't bail, though he might want to. His principles wouldn't allow him to do that. Maybe it was time to set this little guard dog straight, he decided. "One, I don't bail—"

"Ever?" Cindy pressed, her eyes never leaving his face.

"Ever," Dylan told her, his voice firm.

Her own pace increased. She couldn't wait to get out of this claustrophobic passageway. "And two?" she asked him. "You said one, there's got to be at least a second point."

"And two," he continued, "what I was doing

when you accused me of making you walk five paces behind me was plotting strategy."

Cindy looked at him for a long moment, debating whether he was being serious or was just saying what he thought she'd want to hear. She decided to give him the benefit of the doubt. "And how far did you get plotting this strategy?"

Right now, everything in his head was in turmoil. He was searching for the right angle—and also trying to determine why this had blown up on his father at this particular time. Was it just a coincidence? Or was it orchestrated? And, if so, by whom?

But all of these thoughts were still in their infancy and not something he felt up to sharing with anyone. "I'll let you know when I'm ready to."

She knew what that meant. "You don't have anything yet, do you?"

He stopped walking for a second to give her

a penetrating look, then resumed retracing his steps back to Dr. McCallum's basement. "You know, for a woman who likes to keep her own counsel, you certainly feel free to delve into mine."

They both knew she couldn't get anything out of him that he wasn't willing to share. They had that in common. "I can only go as far as you'll let me," she pointed out.

Trouble was, Dylan thought as they worked their way through the last part of the tunnel, he had this sudden, strong desire to share more than just information and strategy with this woman.

Where the hell had that come from, fully dressed and all done up with a bow? A few hours ago, he hadn't even known Cindy Jensen existed and now he was finding himself attracted to the little dictator as well as intrigued by her.

It was probably because she wasn't an open

book the way most of the women he encountered were, Dylan reasoned, trying to understand his motivation. A little while spent in his company and most women he met were willing to disclose anything and everything. Conquests had never been all that challenging for him. And, he assumed, this was the reason these women, attractive though they were, had never held his attention for long.

Just as well. Ultimately, he was a hunter, not a nester.

"I'll keep that in mind," he said as they finally surfaced inside the doctor's basement.

"You want to get something to eat?" Dylan asked Cindy as he was driving her back to the senator's office. It had occurred to him that they'd left the office just before lunch and it was several hours past that now. He knew he could at least stand to grab something to go if not actually sit down to enjoy his meal.

Cindy made no answer.

Was her lack of response supposed to be taken as a no? Glancing in the young woman's direction when her silence continued, he saw that she'd turned possibly the lightest shade of pale he could recall ever having seen on anyone who was still alive and breathing.

It wasn't his imagination. She looked seriously ill. "Are you all right?" he asked, ready either to pull over or to drive straight to the closest available hospital emergency room.

Cindy held up her hand, as if to tell him to hold on because she couldn't answer him immediately.

Damn it, I thought I'd gotten past this part. Obviously not.

It felt as if her entire stomach was threatening to come up. In one continuous wave.

With great effort, Cindy managed to talk herself into keeping the very minor content of her stomach—dry toast and tea, eaten some hours ago—down where it belonged. It was *not* easy. Feeling really ill, she forced herself to swallow. She wasn't about to throw up in this man's car, or even next to it. She'd die first.

Cindy clenched her hands in her lap.

Getting uncomfortably nervous, Dylan cast about for a clue. "Are you carsick?" he asked her.

He remembered that, when they were kids, his sister used to get really carsick unless she sat up front, as close to the driver's side as possible. And even that didn't always help. Trips were prolonged as they pulled over to the side of the road to allow Lana to throw up when her nausea became particularly intense.

He glanced at Cindy again. He'd have thought she was a little old for that. In his experience, most people got over being carsick by the time they were in their late teens or early twenties, but there were always exceptions to everything.

And she definitely looked a little green about the gills. "You want me to pull over?" he offered.

Cindy shook her head, staring straight ahead. Perspiration was gathering along her forehead, blending into her bangs.

"Keep driving," she told him hoarsely. "It'll pass. It was supposed to have passed already."

Given that line of conversation as a clue, Dylan came to the only *other* conclusion he could. "You're pregnant, aren't you?"

A wave of anger, red and hot, swept over him out of nowhere, surprising the hell out of him as it materialized. She was carrying his little half brother or sister, wasn't she?

"Whose baby is it?" he asked for form's sake, even though he figured he already knew the answer to that.

The turmoil in Cindy's stomach settled down to a lesser degree of nausea, one that, while not wonderful, she could at least put up with.

Taking a deep breath, Cindy replayed his question in her head. She thought of flatly denying his overall assumption, but what was the point? She wasn't showing now, but she would be, probably soon, and most likely, if he was pleading his father's case, he'd be around to see her expanding waistline.

"Mine, unfortunately," she answered.

God help her, she wasn't the maternal type. Hadn't even played with dolls as a little girl. What was she going to do with a living, breathing baby?

This was so unfair, but it was the price she paid for not having had the courage to stand up for herself sooner. Who even knew when she would have found her backbone if she hadn't been working for the senator? It was Dean leaving that last mark of his "high regard" for her visible where the senator could see it and express his concern that had infused her with the courage to finally stand up for herself.

The senator had been willing to deal with Dean for her, but she'd insisted on doing it herself, knowing she had to if she was ever going to have any self-respect. So she'd called the police, pressed charges and Dean was taken away. Then she'd filed for divorce—just as she'd found out she was pregnant. From somewhere deep inside, she found the wherewithal to go on.

The senator had been her rock, her source of courage, and she wasn't about to forget it just because he was less than perfect.

Dylan waited for her to say more. At this point, she'd only given him half an answer.

Was his father the father of this woman's baby? He'd seen the two of them interact with one another, not to mention that Cindy Jensen was clearly protective of the senator. And anyone could see that the man had a soft spot for her.

Probably not all he'd had for her, Dylan

thought darkly. Maybe there was even a little love nest somewhere.

"Okay," he allowed. "The baby is obviously yours since you're carrying it. But unless this is another miraculous instance of an immaculate conception, there had to be a male component at a very crucial point in this baby's creation." The ball in her court now, Dylan waited for her to respond.

When she did, it wasn't to say anything he even remotely expected to hear. "That's a popular misconception, you know. No pun intended," Cindy tacked on as her words echoed in her head.

He wasn't following. "What, that a male component is necessary to make a baby?"

"No, that the term *immaculate conception* refers to Mary conceiving Jesus. It actually refers to Mary being conceived without the stain of original sin. Hence—immaculate conception."

She was giving him a religion lesson? She was also stalling, he decided. Why?

"All right, I'm enlightened," he told her. "Enlighten me some more. Are you married?" Dylan decided to start slowly in his subtle interrogation.

She looked down at her left hand. It was still difficult for her to get used to seeing it bare, even though she hadn't been married all that long. She'd just assumed when she'd taken those vows that it would be forever. Just the way she'd assumed that the man she'd fallen in love with would always remain kind and loving, the way he'd been on the day they got married.

Both had turned out to be a lie.

"No, I'm not," she replied, her voice low, distant. Lost.

He gleaned what he could from her tone. Interpreting tones of voice was something he relied on heavily as a lawyer.

"But you were." She slanted a glance in his direction, the look brimming with emotion, with unspoken feelings. She made no response to his assumption. "Oh, c'mon," he coaxed in his best, most charming and enticing manner. He wanted her to do more than give him tightly worded answers. He wanted her to elaborate. "You're not going to leave me just hanging out here like this, are you?"

Her smile was self-contained, revealing nothing. Finally, she gave him an answer. Not the one he wanted. "Yes."

Not to be defeated, Dylan tried another line of questioning. "How far along are you?"

Without realizing it, she glanced down at her flat stomach. At times, she still couldn't get herself to believe it. Her. A mother. This was so wrong. What did she know about mothering? "A lot further than I'm happy about."

She didn't look pregnant, Dylan thought. But, then, he knew that some women didn't, especially not if it was their first pregnancy. One of the other lawyers in the office had a wife who had never showed at all during her first pregnancy until just a week before she gave birth. And even at that point, everyone assumed she'd just gained a little holiday weight.

"There are options, you know," he said, testing the waters gingerly.

"Not if I'm to live with my conscience," she said tersely. "Now, can we talk about the senator instead?" She looked at his profile pointedly. "And don't even *toy* with the idea that this baby is your father's, because it isn't. Your father treats me with the utmost respect which is more than—"

Appalled, Cindy stopped short. She'd almost let the whole story come tumbling out. How could that have happened? She didn't really even know this man. Were hormones responsible for this near lapse of judgment? The most she should ever have considered telling Dylan

Kelley was that his father had offered to stand in her corner if necessary for her to get a divorce from Dean. He'd also offered to get her protection from her controlling husband. She would always, *always* be grateful to the man, even if he had disappointed her so terribly these last few days.

First and foremost, Senator Henry Kelley had been her champion and that was the way she chose to think of him. Now and always.

Chapter 7

"More than what?" Dylan finally prompted when she made no attempt to finish her sentence after stopping practically in midword.

Cindy flashed an apologetic smile as her mind raced for a response. She'd been hoping he'd just let it drop.

"Sorry. I lost my train of thought." She saw he obviously didn't believe her. Not that it was her concern, but it was better if the man didn't think she was just blowing him off, so she elaborated. In a manner of speaking. "That sort of thing happens to pregnant women all the time, so they tell me. They become for-

getful." And then she swiftly turned the conversation in another, more fruitful direction.
"Now, what about the senator? Are you really
going to try to help him, or was that just a lot
of smoke and mirrors?"

Because the traffic was increasing, making
driving trickier, Dylan felt he couldn't risk
looking in her direction. Still, because her
comment mystified him, he had to ask. "To
what end?"

She shrugged, thinking specifically of her
ex-husband who'd gone from being an almost
perfect Dr. Jekyll to a frightening, angry Mr.
Hyde for absolutely no reason. Certainly she
hadn't given him one. But the outcome was
still the same.

"Why does anyone do anything?" she asked.
"Maybe you were just looking for something
to hold over the senator's head for reasons all
your own. Revenge, anger—fill in the right

word. It's up to you." She left the sentence open for him to work with.

Was that how he came across? Dylan wondered. Did she think he was vengeful?

"I meant what I said about helping him because of my mother." And that was all he intended to say in defense of his motives. If he said any more, he felt he'd come across as insincere. "How familiar are you with my father's dealings with the various groups of influence in Congress as well as with the different lobbyists?"

This was familiar territory for her. "Those I'm all up on," she told him. Or was she? "Or, at least I think I am," Cindy felt compelled to qualify. "After being on the receiving end of this sucker punch, I'm not a hundred-percent sure of anything anymore," she had to admit. "Up until this whole media circus started, I thought I was completely in the loop about everything the senator was involved with professionally." An ironic smile curved her mouth. There was no humor in it. "Obviously, though, I wasn't." She looked at him. "Why?"

He went back to one of his sticking points. "Because I'm curious why this is happening at this point in time."

In her opinion, that was simple enough to answer. "Because his bimbo collection decided to come forward."

"But why now?" Dylan emphasized, trying to make her understand his curiosity. "Why not last month? Or last spring? Or this fall?"

She didn't have an answer for that, but was one actually necessary? The end result was still the same: One hell of a scandal. "Does that really matter?" she asked him.

"It might," he replied thoughtfully, working on a knot whose ends were completely hidden to him at this point. He didn't believe in random occurrences or coincidences. Things always happened for a reason. "It just might."

* * *

"Dad, I can come home, stay with you," the young voice on the other end of the cell phone insisted. "You need someone there with you. I'm not going to turn my back on you or pretend everything's all right when it's not."

Despite the humiliating and quite possibly dire situation he found himself in, Hank smiled as he listened to his only daughter's voice. Whatever else he'd done wrong in his life—and the list was becoming rather extensive these days—this much he'd done right. The offspring he'd produced with Sarah were all fine, upstanding young citizens, and none had a bigger heart than Lana, his beautiful little blue-eyed, blond doll.

Not that he'd had much of a hand in anything but his children's initial procreation. Certainly not in raising them. The credit, he freely admitted, all went to his wife, Sarah. He fervently wished that there were such things as do-overs in life. He'd go back and do so many things differently this time. Learn to treasure the good things that life had given him instead of questing for more.

But there were no do-overs. There was only now and the future—if he managed to live through this mess to see it. All he could do was hope that things would work themselves out so that he would get the opportunity to make it up to all of them, especially to Sarah. If she let him.

"I appreciate that, Lana, I really do. But I want you to stay in Europe. Keep up with your studies," he urged. God knew he'd disrupted enough lives without disrupting hers as well. "I can't have you coming here." Even as he told her to stay away, he was making up his mind that he was going to have to go some-where else. Away from here. And the less Lana knew about his plans, the less of a liability she was. To herself *and* to him. "It's not safe being around me right now."

"Not safe?" Lana echoed, confused and a little afraid for her father at the same time. "What do you mean it's not safe? Dad, what's going on?" she cried nervously. "Please tell me."

Hank had always had a quick, fertile mind. It was one of the reasons the Society had singled him out in the first place. He thought quickly now, searching for a plausible lie to feed his daughter. There was absolutely no point in her worrying about him. His previous wording had been a bad slip of the tongue on his part. He was going to have to be more careful in the future.

"I meant as in my reputation being blackened the way it is. I don't want it rubbing off on you and if the public sees you standing by me, that's exactly what'll happen."

At twenty-four, things like reputations carried little significance to Lana. "I don't care about my reputation, Dad," she insisted. "What I care about is you."

"Very flattering, dear. I am touched." And he was, but he needed to make her understand. "But you *need* to care about your reputation. In the end, that's all any of us has—our reputations, our legacy."

And *he* should have thought of that earlier, he upbraided himself. He was acutely aware of that now. But that was all water under a very shaky proverbial bridge, he thought in despair.

"Listen, sweetheart, the best thing you can do for me is make sure you and your mother keep out of the public eye. Go somewhere where the media can't get to you." And nobody else, either, he added silently.

He couldn't tell his daughter outright what he was afraid of. He had only his suspicions to guide him and they might turn out to be all wrong. He might, with any luck, be overreacting. Besides, he didn't want to frighten Lana.

Didn't want her thinking that her own life was in danger because of something he had gotten mixed up in.

This was what he got for being so damn full of himself, Hank thought now. He'd allowed his hubris to get the better of him and now he was being punished. That, in itself, he could make his peace with. He'd done a lot of bad things in his time and he deserved to be metaphorically lynched in public for it. But the other, the other had been a matter of being flattered that such high-ranking men wanted him as part of their ultra-secret, do-not-breathe-a-word-of-this organization, Raven's Head Society.

His inherent insecurities always had him hunting for validation. But fifteen minutes into the initial get-acquainted meeting, once the euphoria about rubbing elbows with these men, all famous for one reason or another, had worn off, he'd realized that he was in way over his head. But bowing out as he wanted to was severely frowned upon. He'd found that out when they'd taken a vote on what he'd initially assumed was actually a joke.

He'd discovered this very quickly and had also discovered that the other members of this "gathering" didn't like their members, especially their *new* members, taking a pass on something that required every member's seal of approval.

Words like *treason* and *betrayal* had been bandied about. All pointedly aimed at him.

He'd walked out of that meeting turned around one hundred and eighty degrees from the man he'd been going in. Going in he'd been positive, enthusiastic. Hopeful. And pretty damn full of himself.

That had quickly changed when he'd realized what it was that they, these captains of industry, congressmen, renowned surgeons and figures from the world arena, were proposing.

It was something so outlandish, so horrific, that even now he didn't want to think about it or dwell on the consequences its commission would have.

Once done, the repercussions would encompass not just this country but the world as well. And the greater good they claimed they were focusing on was only *their* greater good. For, down to the man, they would all profit from this.

Greedy though he was, Hank knew he had to draw the line somewhere. And this was where he drew it.

But he didn't want to have to stand and defend his position. He was only one man and, as such, he now realized, insignificant in their eyes. They'd roll right over him.

And maybe worse.

That was when he'd known he had to make himself scarce. Really scarce. That meant that he had to get away from his family estate as well. This location wasn't safe for him. It was too well-known.

A chill ran down his spine.

Those reporters camped outside his gates— who was to say that there wasn't a messenger from the Society among them? Someone with one final, silencing message.

He needed to go.

Almost as much as he needed to keep his family, especially his daughter and his wife, safe.

He realized that Lana was talking to him. "I'm sorry, honey, I didn't hear that," he apologized. "What did you just say?"

"I said I want to be with you," Lana insisted. "You need someone in your corner."

"I have someone," he assured her.

For a moment, there was silence on the other end. And then Lana asked him in a still voice. "One of *them*?"

He heard the contempt in each word. Lana

might be the light of his life, but she was also her mother's daughter, he thought. He didn't blame either one of them. He blamed only himself.

"No," he told her. "It's your brother, Dylan. He said he was going to help me mount a defense, take on my case."

This time, the moment of silence was followed by a question echoing with disbelief. "Dylan came to see you?" she asked incredulously.

"That's what I just said," Hank told his youngest, his voice filled with all the affection he felt for her. "So there's no need for you to come rushing here and turn yourself into a target—for the media's slings and arrows," he tagged on quickly.

He was badly rattled, he thought. Otherwise, he wouldn't be so careless with his words. If he frightened her, she might not be able to think clearly and might not take the precautions she needed to in order to stay out of the Society's line of vision. He didn't want them getting any ideas.

"I'll feel a lot better knowing you and your mother are safe and out of harm's way," he concluded.

It was obvious that Lana thought he meant metaphorically. "Mom's pretty upset by all this, you know," she told him, lowering her voice a little. It made him wonder if perhaps Sarah was somewhere close by, near their daughter. Had she flown to Paris, seeking to escape the scandal he'd brought down on them all?

The guilt he felt for having hurt his wife did hang heavily on him now, although he doubted that anyone would believe him. He'd never started out to hurt anyone. He'd just wanted to enjoy himself and wield as much power as he could. Somehow it had all escalated, getting out of hand, and it was now coming back to haunt him, demanding its pound of flesh in exchange.

Everything, Hank now realized wearily, had consequences.

"Yes, I know," he said to Lana. "Listen, baby, tell your mother I'm sorry. Tell her that I never meant for any of this to hurt her."

"Um," Lana felt uncomfortable. Not with the request, but with what she assumed her father hoped to accomplish by extending an apology through her. "I don't think she really wants to hear from you right now, Dad."

He couldn't blame Sarah, he thought. "Tell her anyway," he requested. "Just so she knows." Though he realized it was overkill, his concern made him emphasize his plea one last time. "And make sure that you stay somewhere off the grid. And keep safe."

"Dad, you're scaring me."

Damn, he had to learn to curb his mouth, he upbraided himself. It was going to bring about his ultimate downfall one day—if it hadn't already. If he listened rather than talked, maybe none of this would be happening right now.

"Nothing to be scared of, baby," he assured her. "Just do as I say. Promise?"

"Promise," he heard her say reluctantly.

As he hung up, Hank told himself that at least he had that to cling to.

That, and the integrity of his sons. It was more, he realized, than he deserved.

Squaring his shoulders, he went to pack. And to make fresh plans.

"Are you going to get in contact with him?" Bonnie Gene finally demanded of her husband, unable to hold her tongue any longer.

Donald didn't answer her.

She'd tried to wait it out, expecting her husband to do the right thing. She'd given Donald his space, let him putter around the restaurant's damn kitchen right through into the wee hours of the morning as he supposedly worked on yet another secret sauce—a sauce the world did *not* need since their restaurant chain already had many other "secret sauces" currently in use and responsible for the return of legions of customers to their tables time and again.

But instead of finally coming around and doing the right thing, the way she'd hoped, Donald had just sunk deeper into silence.

Well, she'd had enough of playing the patient, understanding wife. It was damn well time for the man to live up to his responsibilities as the head of this large extended family.

Telling herself to be patient, Bonnie Gene tried again. "Donald, I'm talking to you. When are you going to call Hank?"

His solid form partially wrapped in an apron splattered with a variety of different stains representing a host of ingredients, Donald barely glanced up from the huge pot that corralled his attention. He knew that if he didn't glance up, there would be hell to pay. Bonnie Gene could be a force to be reckoned with when she got going.

"I'm not," was all he said before returning to his culinary work in progress.

The new sauce didn't taste right and he blamed that on Hank. If he wasn't so preoccupied, so wrapped up in trying *not* to be wrapped up in his half brother's dilemma, his head would be clear enough for him to concentrate on what he was supposed to be doing. After all, this was their bread and butter.

Hands on her still-trim hips, Bonnie Gene tossed her head, loosening the French twist that held her shoulder-length dark-brown hair in place. She deliberately got between her exasperating husband and the giant pot on the stove that had his attention so annoyingly riveted.

"Hank is family," she pointed out sternly.

"He's an idiot," Donald snapped in barely

suppressed anger, circling around his wife to get at the stove from a different angle.

Not to be outdone—or outmaneuvered—Bonnie Gene turned around to face him. "Doesn't matter. He's still family."

Bonnie Gene knew she didn't have to explain to her husband how she felt about the responsibilities that went with that kind of a tie. She firmly believed that you didn't just stick by a person when times were good and there was something to be gained from being in their light. You stuck by them most of all when they needed you and things were at their darkest.

"Bonnie and Clyde had families," Donald pointed out, grumbling. "Don't recall ever reading that either of their families tried to help them out when the law was after them."

"Don't exaggerate, Donald," she told him tersely. "It's not the same thing."

Donald stopped stirring and put the extra-long wooden spoon down so hard, the noise echoed through the kitchen. "Exaggerating?" he repeated, a frown on his otherwise cherubic face. "I thought I was downplaying it. Look, Hank's been playing fast and loose all his life. *He* was the favorite son. *He* was the one who got all the advantages, all the attention. *He* always pushed the envelope to the edge and beyond, thinking he was bullet-proof. *He* really believed that for him, there were no consequences. Well, guess what? There are. He's a big boy now, and he needs to take his lumps just like the rest of us."

Bonnie Gene knew that shouting at her husband wasn't going to get her anywhere. He needed to be cajoled into doing the right thing. Bullying had never worked with Donald. So she struggled with her temper as she appealed to his softer side. After all, it was Donald—by his own choice—who'd been the surrogate father to Hank's boys while his brother had run for office and whatever else had suited his fancy at the time. Now it was time for him to be a father figure to his brother as well.

"But he's not like the rest of us, Donald. He's definitely not strong, the way you are. I'm not telling you to take those lumps for him, I'm asking you to let the man know that he's not alone in this. That his big brother is there to stand by him if he needs him."

But this time, Donald refused to be swayed. He felt around in his pocket, ready to light up one of his ever-present cigars, the ones his wife took such joy in removing from between his lips. But this time, he'd forgotten to put one into his pocket to take the place of the one Bonnie Gene had destroyed yesterday.

He was going to have to wait until she left the kitchen to get at his secret stash, he thought, irritated. "If you're that worried about him, *you* call him and tell him that *you're* there for him."

Bonnie Gene shook her head. Why was

Donald being so stubborn? "It's not the same thing."

"It'll have to do because it's the only thing Hank's going to hear from this side of the family," he said dismissively. He picked up the wooden spoon again and went back to stirring.

"You're not going to call him?" she asked, stunned that he was still refusing her request. Usually, he would have given in by now, especially when he sensed how much this meant to her.

"I'm not going to call him," Donald confirmed, keeping his eyes on his simmering sauce.

Bonnie Gene threw up her hands. Swallowing a few choice words about the similarity between her husband and a baboon, she left the kitchen before she said something they were both *really* going to regret.

The moment she was gone—one eye on the door at all times—Donald went to retrieve a much-needed cigar.

Chapter 8

Dylan's plan was to drop Cindy back at her office and then proceed to his late-afternoon appointment. But a call from his client, begging off because of a family emergency and requesting to reschedule, had Dylan changing his plans.

Instead of simply dropping Cindy off, he decided to stop to get lunch, albeit a late one, to go. He left the choice up to her. Without hesitation she opted for Chinese food, specifically, egg drop soup, something she'd discovered by accident helped settle her less-than-calm stomach.

"Chinese it is," he said.

He knew of a place that served above-average food not that far from his father's office. Once he got their order and was back in the car, she had to ask. "You're coming back to the office with me? Because it doesn't look as if you're planning on just depositing me back where you found me," she explained, nodding at the take-out bag on the floor.

"Sharp lady," he said. Stopping at a red light, he turned toward Cindy and asked, "Are you up for helping me?"

Despite the fact that Dylan's magnetic blue eyes completely had her attention, her mistake of a marriage to Dean had taught her never to agree to anything unless she was first clear on all the particulars. "Help you do what?"

He would have thought that was self-explanatory. "Save your boss's hide."

Amusement curved her mouth. "Put so very eloquently, how can I possibly refuse?"

Not that she would, no matter how he put it. If there was a way to help the senator, she wanted to be part of it, part of clearing his name as much as possible. "What is it that you have in mind?"

Something I shouldn't. The thought floated through his head in response to her question, completely out of left field.

Well, maybe not so completely, Dylan silently amended. He'd always had a weakness for pretty faces and hers was definitely pretty. More than pretty. Not only that, but she also struck him as a lady who wouldn't give him any cause for concern. She didn't seem to be a woman who was after a relationship or who would grab on to a man just because she wanted to accessorize her life.

The truth was, the fact that she wasn't interested *him.*

This wasn't going to help his father any, Dylan reminded himself. And that was, after all, why he was here in the first place. Anything on the side would have to remain that way for now, to be revisited once he got things organized and in some kind of operative order. That and damage control had to be his twin priorities. Exploring Cindy Jensen's psyche—and whatever else she'd let him explore—could be his reward for a job well done.

"I want to figure out why my father's the focal point of an attack right now. Maybe there's someone out there who has something to gain by bringing him down at this particular time. If so, if we can find out who and why, we can get at the heart of all this. If we can separate the truth from the lies, maybe, just maybe, we can save the old man from being convicted of anything other than exercising some incredibly poor judgment." The light had turned green and they were moving again. "So, are you up for it?"

He debated asking if she'd just rather go

home and rest instead, but he had a feeling that she'd take that as an insult, so he kept the last part to himself.

"I'm up for it," she replied. "But I'm curious." She'd gotten the sense, perhaps wrongly, that Dylan Kelley liked to do things alone, the Lone Ranger of lawyers. Of course, she reminded herself, the Lone Ranger did have a sidekick, a Native American who had nursed him back to health after finding him left for dead by a band of outlaws. Was Dylan picking her to be his Tonto? "Why me?"

She saw him struggle not to smile. "You're his Chief Staff Assistant, remember?"

He was mocking her, wasn't he? "I remember," she replied quietly in a voice that couldn't be read.

Something alerted him to tread lightly. He went with the truth, rather than flattery. "The way I see it, you know his schedule, the names of the people he interacts with during the course of the day, the week, the month. Unless I'm mistaken, you're pretty much up on his entire professional life. Somewhere in there is someone with something to gain from my father's fall from grace in the public arena. I need you to help me figure out who that someone is."

He made a good case, but then, she would have expected nothing less from the way he presented himself. "Makes sense."

He slanted her a look just as he pulled into the underground parking structure beneath her office building. "Glad you approve."

This one was going to keep her on her toes, Cindy thought. Right now, that was something she welcomed. It would distract her from being both disappointed in and concerned about the senator. She never liked the prospect of being at loose ends, especially not now, not when her future, both personal and professional, looked so uncertain.

* * *

They had only been at work in the senator's office for a little less than an hour when Dylan's cell phone rang. Several selected bars of Beethoven's "Moonlight Sonata" filled the air around them.

He saw the amused look on Cindy's face as he took his cell out. She looked younger when she smiled, he thought. Like a teenager instead of the woman in her early thirties that he knew her to be.

"What?"

She shook her head in response. She was going to have to get better at keeping a poker face, she thought. "Nothing. I just don't picture you as the classical-music type."

The truth was that he liked all sorts of music, but classical music was what his mother enjoyed and whenever he heard it, he thought of her. And his childhood. That had been a damn sight easier than adult life was turning out to be.

"I'm a man of many layers, Cindy," he told her with a wink.

The wink went right through her, rousing unsettling feelings like a two-second earthquake. "So it would seem," she murmured, wondering what she might find if she peeled back a layer or two.

The very idea that the thought had remotely crossed her mind brought her to an abrupt mental halt. Just what was going on with her head today? This wasn't like her. She wasn't given to thinking about men, handsome or otherwise. She'd realized that she was an incredibly bad judge of character and no man turned out to be what he seemed. If she had any doubts about that, thinking that maybe Dean had been an isolated case, all she had to do was look to the senator to show her that she was wrong.

Had to be her hormones talking, she decided.

Pregnant women, she'd learned, were subject to fluctuating hormones. She had to be careful not to let herself be ambushed by them, allowing them to make her do something stupid. She also had to remember that *finally,* she was in control of her own life.

Sort of, she amended ruefully, looking down at her stomach accusingly.

Dylan missed the rainbow of emotions passing over Cindy's face as she thought her situation through. He'd turned his back toward her as he took the incoming call on his cell. The number was utterly unfamiliar at first glance.

"Dylan Kelley," he said by way of a greeting, then waited for a response.

"Mr. Kelley," The female voice on the other end was breathless, as if the woman had run across a football field to place this call. "This is Martha. I'm sorry to bother you, but you did tell me to call if I saw something out of the ordinary."

Dylan stiffened. He'd said that to his father's housekeeper in passing as he left. He certainly hadn't expected her to call so soon.

Had something happened to his father?

Maybe he shouldn't have been so cavalier in leaving the estate without thoroughly checking the security system first.

"Is something wrong, Martha?"

"I think so." The woman lowered her voice, as if afraid she would be overheard making the call. "I thought you should know that the senator seems to be packing up his belongings."

His father had seemed a little restless, but he hadn't said anything about leaving the estate. Had something happened in the last hour? "Where's he going?"

"That I do not know, sir, but it appears to be away from here. He's taking a lot of things." She paused, uncertain at her own intrusion. "You did say to call if anything unusual occurred," she repeated nervously.

"And I'm grateful you did. I'll be right there," he told the housekeeper.

But not before I call the old man first, he added silently.

"Something wrong?" Cindy asked, alerted by the shift in Dylan's tone as he talked to whoever had called him.

"Apparently the old man's making a break for it," he said as he quickly hit the number he'd preprogrammed earlier, after Cindy had given him his father's cell phone number.

"A break? For where?" Cindy wanted to know.

Dylan shrugged in response, since he hadn't a clue. She would probably know the answer to that better than he would. He had no idea who his father called a friend these days.

The next second he raised his hand, silently asking her to hold her thoughts. His father had picked up on the other end.

"Where are you going, Dad?" he asked in response to his father's uncertain greeting.

"How did you know?" Hank demanded, the ever-growing paranoia clearly evident in his voice.

"That's beside the point," Dylan said, refusing to be sidetracked. "You can't just take off like this. You're not some carefree kid who can just disappear when he wants to. Where are you going?"

There was frustration in his father's voice as he answered, "I don't know yet."

His father had struck Dylan as barely hanging on when he'd left him earlier. If the man took off now, who knew where he would wind up? Not to mention that he had to be able to get hold of his father when the need arose.

"You have to have a plan in place, Dad." Dylan stopped himself. He didn't need to be told that his father wouldn't welcome a lecture right now—at least, not from him. "Sit tight until I get to you," Dylan instructed. "I'm coming right over." When his father made no response to either statement, Dylan asked, "Did you hear me, Dad?"

"Yes, I heard you. Just hurry. You said you'd be right over?"

Okay, something was definitely off. Why was the man acting so strangely? "Did something happen after I left?" Dylan wanted to know.

"No," the senator snapped. Agitated, he added, "But it might. It just might."

"I'll be right there," Dylan promised again. "Just don't leave." With that, he closed his cell and dropped it into the pocket of his jacket.

"What's wrong?" Cindy hadn't bothered even pretending that she wasn't listening in. The concerned look on Dylan's face only made matters worse.

"Something's got the old man spooked," Dylan told her. "I'm going back to see him." He saw that she had risen as well. "Going home?" But even as he made the query, he had a feeling that wasn't it.

"Going with you," she corrected, getting her purse.

He gave it one shot. "There's no need for you to go back to the estate—"

Cindy cut him off. "I'll be the judge of that. If the senator's upset enough to want to take off again, there's definitely a need for me to go with you. You admitted that you two are practically strangers. Neither one of you looked comfortable with the other earlier. The senator needs a friendly face to talk to."

He never liked being kept in the dark. "Look, I have no right to ask, but what is it between you and my father?" he wanted to know. "It's definitely something more than just a boss and his assistant."

She looked at him for a long moment. He found he couldn't even make an educated guess what was going on behind those deep-brown eyes of hers.

"You're right," she finally said.

He had no idea why being right caused his stomach to drop. "It's something more?"

"No, you have no right to ask," she told him crisply. "Listening to your end of the conversation, I got the impression that time was of the essence, so let's not waste any more than we already have, okay?" She looked at him pointedly. "Let's go."

"Ever consider being a drill sergeant?" he asked, amused despite himself. "You seem to have a natural aptitude for it."

"I'll put it on the list of future jobs to look into," she answered, leading the way out.

Ordinarily, Dylan wouldn't have dropped everything this way. He would have attempted to calm his father down over the phone, but the senior Kelley had seemed too agitated. The man had also given him the feeling that he was too unpredictable to leave to his own devices, obviously upset and growing more so. Dylan felt they needed to see each other face to face again to get to the bottom of what was going on. He was still fairly certain that he could tell if his father was lying.

Was Hank having a breakdown of sorts, confronted with a situation he had no control over? Dylan wondered as he drove over. Or was there something else at work here? Something that hadn't come to light yet? Was there a reason why Hank Kelley was behaving so erratically?

He needed to look into his father's eyes as they spoke to get a better feel for what was going on. It was obvious he hadn't entirely leveled with his son earlier.

No surprise there, Dylan thought cryptically.

This time, they didn't bother taking a roundabout route. In the interest of brevity, they entered through the front gates, passing the wall of reporters, all clamoring for a statement of some sort, a sound bite to run with.

Dylan never slowed his vehicle down, never looked at a single face. Instead, he stonily kept his face forward, his gaze on his target, focused on the estate proper as he drove toward it.

Distant flashes of light accompanied their disembar-kation from the vehicle as the tabloid contingent with their incredibly long-range lenses took photograph after photograph to commemorate and freeze their arrival—until the next big scandal came along.

Taking Cindy's arm, Dylan acted as a human buffer, placing himself between his father's assistant and the cameras. He felt her instantly stiffen; he pretended not to notice.

"Don't look at them," he ordered.

He sounded so deadly serious, she had to laugh. Or maybe that was just tension arising from the hold he had on her arm. She had to remind herself he wasn't Dean.

And she was never going to give him the opportunity to *become* Dean.

"Or what?" she asked. "I'll turn into a pillar of salt?"

"No, but you'll have your face splashed across God knows how many tabloid rags and most likely the evening cable news as well, heralding you as yet another one of my father's mistresses, brazenly come to comfort him in his time of need."

Her eyes widened as she stared at him incredulously. He hustled her to the front door. "But I'm not," Cindy protested.

He shook his head. "Doesn't matter. They'll still call you that. Didn't you know? When it comes to scandals, you're guilty until proven innocent."

"So then why didn't we use the tunnel again?" she asked.

Yeah, maybe he should have after all. But it was too late for that now.

"Because I wanted to give them a show of family solidarity," he told her. "I thought it might do the old man some good, seeing *that* on the evening news. I'm beginning to regret it," he admitted. He didn't bother with the obvious answer, that this route was also, ultimately, faster than finding their way underground.

She glossed over the last part, taking, what to her was the only thing that really meant something here. "So you do care about him," she concluded with a touch of triumph.

Dylan honestly didn't know if he was capable of having feelings for his father. It had been a very long time since he'd felt anything when it came to the old man, but one thing he did know. "I don't like seeing the media torture anyone unless it happens to be a proven first-degree murderer."

She paused to smile at him as he rang the

doorbell. "There goes my theory about all lawyers being cold-blooded reptiles."

"Don't throw it out just yet," he advised wryly. "You might want to dust it off again soon enough."

Her eyebrows came together over her near-perfect nose. "Why?"

He had no time to answer, the front door was opening. Martha stood on the other side, looking very concerned. Gone was the friendly smile, replaced by one continuous frown line.

"He's still upstairs, packing," she told Dylan. "I'm glad you came so quickly. It would be a shame if he did something rash. Those vultures out there," she nodded toward the winding road and the gates beyond it, "want nothing more than to rip him to shreds."

"I think the time for worrying about his doing something rash is past, Martha. All we can do is try to keep him from making it worse," Dylan told her.

He walked into the foyer, its brighter-than-bright chandelier bathing the entire area in what seemed like warm sunlight. Dylan went directly to the dual staircase, taking the side closest to him. At the foot, he paused to look at Cindy.

"You can stay down here if you want to," he told her.

She read between the lines. He didn't want her tiring herself out or exerting herself. He was being protective. Why? What was his angle? Dean had taught her that no man was nice just for the sake of being nice. There was always a motive, an ultimate plan.

"Exercise is supposed to be good for me," she told him.

Almost against her will, even as she set up barriers of denial about her condition, she'd glanced through the reading material her gynecologist had placed in her hands the day she'd confirmed her pregnancy.

"You'll want to take care of yourself and your baby," Dr. Sutherland had told her. The woman's words still rang in Cindy's ears, cropping up every day or so, driving her crazy. She didn't want this baby. What did she know about raising a baby? Her own mother was dead by the time she was four and her father had put her into the foster system, saying he just wasn't up to taking care of a little girl. She had no role models, no base to start from. This unborn child was a disaster waiting to happen.

She forced herself to focus on the situation before her. "Just lead the way," she told Dylan, waving him up first.

The suite that served as his father's bedroom—connected to his mother's bedroom by two oversize walk-in closets placed back to back—was in the center of the second floor. The door was standing open, but Dylan knocked on it anyway just before entering.

His father had his back to the entrance, absorbed by the frustrating activity of trying to fit an enormous amount of clothing into a regular-size suitcase.

"I take it you don't pack your own suitcases very often," Dylan commented.

His father swung around, all the blood suddenly draining from his face. His complexion had turned to a ghostly shade of chalk in the course of one heartbeat. His hand now splayed across his chest, he glared at his son.

"Dylan, you scared the hell out of me," he cried.

"Apparently." Why was the man so spooked? "For the record, I knocked. And I have a witness." He nodded at Cindy. "Where're you going, Dad?"

The senator ran his hand through his silver mane. "Away."

"Anything more specific than that?" The blank look on his father's face answered the question for him. "Just what I thought," Dylan said with a sigh. He had his work cut out for him. His father was coming apart.

Chapter 9

It took patience and time, but Dylan finally managed to persuade his father to remain at the estate until he could make arrangements for the man to stay somewhere safe and far off the grid. The deciding factor had been a promise to find him a bodyguard, one who necessarily came from outside the system and had no ties to any of the people who lived within the world of politics and power that the senator, until a few days ago, had inhabited.

One of the two men he'd been thinking of bringing in, Bart Holden, had already been contacted and had agreed to take the job. The one he really wanted, though, was an ex-special ops agent named Gage Prescott. However, he had yet to be contacted and brought in. He knew Gage by reputation, knew that the man was fearless and capable of putting his life on the line in order to protect whomever he had sworn to protect. Right now, Dylan had a gut feeling that was *exactly* the kind of man his father needed guarding him.

Off the top of his head, Dylan didn't know how long finding Gage would take, given that he had no idea where the man currently might be.

In the interim, Dylan told his pacing father that he would call in a favor from a local private investigator he knew and trusted to stay at the estate until he got other things into place.

"What things?" Hank had asked nervously.

"It's better that you not know that until everything's set," Dylan had replied.

That his father had readily agreed with him

showed Dylan just how far the man had fallen. The old Senator Kelley would have never allowed control of his own fate to be taken away like that.

It also told Dylan that his instincts were right. There was something else wrong, something else going on that his father hadn't disclosed, and that he remained, as of yet, entirely unwilling to acknowledge or talk about.

"He said the reporters were responsible for making him so jumpy," Dylan told Cindy as, once again, he drove her back to his father's office. This time he only intended to drop Cindy off in the underground parking facility so that she could retrieve her car and go home.

Listening to Dylan, she picked up on his skeptical tone. "You don't buy it," she guessed.

Rather than answer directly, he glanced at her as he asked, "Do you?"

The question didn't require any thought on her part. "No," she admitted.

The senator's present behavior was completely out of character for the man she had come to know and regard as a surrogate father.

Dylan was glad he wasn't the only one who felt that there was something else going on. "I've seen him with reporters. My father charms them, uses them. And he is pretty much in contempt of them. They *don't* have this kind of effect on him. They don't make him jumpy. There's something else going on here, something he doesn't want to talk about."

Cindy nodded. "I know. I'm beginning to feel the same way." She sighed. "So, if he won't tell you, what are you going to do?"

"Well, I can't exactly tie him to a chair and use a rubber hose on the man to get him to talk." He banked down his growing frustration. "I suppose I just have to wait and try to get him to trust me enough to confide in me. Unless—"

The last word just hung in the air. "Unless what?" Cindy prodded.

It was suddenly so simple. Dylan slanted a glance at her. "My father trusts you. Maybe if you try to get him to tell you what it is that has him so nervous that every single noise has him jumping and looking over his shoulder…"

They were stopped at a red light. Dylan's voice had trailed off and she assumed it was because he was waiting for her to tell him that she'd do what he'd just suggested. But when she looked at him, she saw that he was regarding her with an expression that told her he was thinking of something else.

Weighing something else.

She snatched up the unfinished sentence, hoping to distract him from whatever path his thoughts were taking in regards to her. "Well, I don't know if it'll work, but I can certainly try to get the senator to open up."

The light turned green. Dylan took his foot

off the brake and looked back at the road. "How about you?"

For reasons she wasn't completely clear about, her pulse accelerated faster than the car did. "How about me what?"

"What can I do or say to make *you* open up?"

Where had that come from? And, more importantly, where was he going with this?

"This isn't about me," Cindy pointed out tersely. She didn't want him invading her private life, probing and prodding it as if it was something he had the right to dissect. Because he didn't. No one did.

Dylan guided the car into the underground parking facility. "No, but in your own way you're as tense as he is. You're jumpy," he added, using the same word he'd used to describe his father's jittery nerves. "Why?"

She tossed her hair back, looking straight ahead. "You're imagining things."

"No, I'm not." And they both knew it. "Every

time I touch any part of you, an arm, a shoulder, if I just accidentally brush by you, you either tense up as stiff as a baton or you flinch. Unless you're allergic to me, or have the world's most delicate skin, there's only one reason for you to react that way."

"That's my car, over there," she pointed out, hoping to terminate this third degree he was subjecting her to. She should have known better.

Instead of driving toward her parked vehicle, Dylan pulled his own over to the side. Bringing it to a dead stop, he hit the door locks, forcing her to remain inside. He looked at her and saw panic flash in her eyes. It proved his theory and made him feel guilty for putting her through this. But ultimately, he wasn't the one who had created the basis for her fears.

He had his suspicions who had, but he didn't want to jump to any conclusions. "Who hurt you, Cindy?" he asked softly.

She set her mouth hard, refusing to look at him. "I have no idea what you're talking about."

He didn't have any patience to play games, but for her sake, he dug deep for whatever patience he did have.

"You're too intelligent to act dumb," he told her. "Women who automatically flinch when someone raises a hand or touches them are victims of abuse. Who was it?" She didn't answer but Dylan refused to drop the subject. This was bigger than any need to remain polite. "Was it the baby's father?"

Her head jerked up. Rather than fear, or a deer-in-the-headlights look, he saw indignant anger. Good, it meant that whoever had done this to her hadn't completely crushed her spirit.

"He's not a father," Cindy cried heatedly. Her eyes filled with tears even as she berated herself for being so weak as to allow her emotions to get the better of her. But when she became passionate about something, her control over tears waned. This despite the fact that the complete wasted mass of skin and blood vessels that was her ex wasn't worth her tears. "He's a monster." She whispered the word, afraid that if she said it any louder, her voice would crack and then she really would cry.

He was right, although he felt no satisfaction in the fact. Her ex-husband *had* abused her. "Does he know he's going to be a father?" He was guessing the answer to that was no, but he wanted to hear her verification.

Cindy took a breath, then shook her head. "I want no contact with the man. I took out a restraining order against him before I ever filed for divorce. Your father helped me get it," she told him. "The senator made a few calls and got it fast-tracked. I don't know what I would have done without him."

Dylan was beginning to understand the nature of the relationship between his father and this woman. The old man had taken an interest in his assistant the way he should have done with his own family years ago. Maybe this was his way of atoning.

"Besides," she added, her voice still low, but slowly shedding the pain that enshrouded it, "Dean—my ex—always hated kids. The thought of having one of his own would have made him want to skip town and leave the country. There's no way he'd pay child support. Nor would I want him to. Trust me, the man is *not* daddy material."

That wasn't surprising. "Most men aren't, at least not to start with."

She couldn't believe what she was hearing. "You're actually *defending* him?"

Defending an abuser was the last thing he'd do. To him, anyone who abused a woman or a child was the lowest life form possible. "No, I'm not defending him. I'm just stating a relatively obvious fact. Women are the nurturers.

Men are the hunters and gatherers, the providers."

That got under her skin, rousing her anger and she was secretly grateful for it. "Do you come with your own loincloth and club or will one be provided for you at your local cave?" she wanted to know.

Good, she'd bounced back from that momentary lapse. He'd seen the tears and had felt guilty about them. Now he could leave her for the night without feeling as if he was walking away from someone who was exceedingly vulnerable. He wouldn't have felt right about doing that.

"I haven't checked my membership literature about that yet. I'll let you know when I find out," he promised, doing his best not to grin. His success was only marginal.

Rather than hitting the lock release, he started up his car again and drove her over to her car.

"You didn't have to do that," she told him. "I could have walked."

"I know," he replied. "I wanted to do this. It's dark and there aren't that many cars left here. It's not safe for a pretty woman to be walking around here alone."

He was being nice. God, she wished she could let her guard down enough to just enjoy that. But she couldn't. Everything was suspect to her now. Every nice gesture extended by a man could be a potential smoke screen to lull her into a feeling of complacency—and then he'd turn the tables on her.

When they'd met, Dean had seemed like the embodiment of an earthbound guardian angel. He'd turned out to be the devil in disguise once they were married.

"What's going to happen to him?" she asked Dylan.

He knew she was asking about his father. Dylan didn't try to snow her. He had a feeling she'd see right through it and wouldn't appreciate the gesture. She was more likely to be insulted by it.

"That all depends on what he's really done. And whose persona non grata list he's on. Finding out is going to take a lot of digging." Especially since his father wasn't offering any clues.

Nodding, Cindy told him, "You're going to need help with that digging."

Dylan was well aware of that. In the time they'd spent in his father's office today, they hadn't begun to scrape the surface. "You volunteering?"

She caught her lower lip between her teeth. Was she making a mistake, agreeing to work beside this man? But if she didn't, who would help him? The rest of the staff had made themselves scarce, waiting for this to play itself out.

"I'm volunteering."

For a moment, he thought of just going upstairs to his father's office and picking up where they'd left off. Doubling back to the estate and attempting to calm the man down had bitten a large chunk out of their time. But it was getting late and he still had at least a couple of phone calls to make on his father's behalf. He needed to set things in motion.

"I can pick you up at your place tomorrow morning," he told her. She looked as if she was hesitating. He took a guess as to why. "If you're worried about telling me where you live, I already know."

She looked surprised even though she told herself she shouldn't be. He was the senator's son. It seemed to be a requirement for a Kelley to know as much about everything he was dealing with as he could. Still, she had to ask. "How? You just met me."

"I have ways at my disposal," he answered. "And I could have lied and told you I didn't know. Honesty should count for something."

It should, she thought. And, intellectually, it did. But her nerves didn't run on intellect. Her emotions were directly connected to that pipeline.

Still, under normal circumstances, he did have a point. "It does," she finally conceded. Opening the car door on her side, she got out. They were just feet away from her car; still, she automatically looked around, making sure that Dean wasn't lurking somewhere in the shadows.

It looked as if she was in a Dean-free zone, she thought with a sigh of relief. Stepping back, she said, "I'll see you tomorrow."

He nodded, then opened his window as she walked past him. "Nine o'clock all right?"

She was an early riser, always had been. Marriage and the need to have everything prepared just so had reinforced her natural tendencies.

"Why not eight?"

"Eight it is," he agreed, stifling a yawn. It had been one hell of a long day. And it wasn't over yet.

The sound of her heels clicking against the concrete echoed around the near-empty parking level. Now that she was out of his car, she expected Dylan to drive away. But he didn't. Not until she'd reached her car, released the security alarm and gotten in. Only when she started her car did she see him pull away.

Was he watching over her? Or just watching her?

Again, she damned Dean for having destroyed her ability to simply enjoy something without feeling the need to take it apart and examine it from every angle, overanalyzing it as she searched for the flaw.

Tomorrow, she thought. In the immortal, albeit fictitious, words of Scarlett O'Hara (or Little Orphan Annie), she'd think about it tomorrow.

* * *

The first call Dylan made when he arrived home was to Gage Prescott, the ex-special-ops agent who was currently in the bodyguard-for-hire business. He couldn't believe his luck when Gage answered the phone almost immediately. And the fickle goddess, Lady Luck, hadn't exhausted her supply of fairy dust with that. The man had just come off a major assignment and was already looking for his next job.

Conveniently devoid of any family ties, Gage could be mobile within a relatively short amount of time. That was a big plus in Dylan's book.

He didn't have to tiptoe around the bodyguard or sugarcoat anything. Gage took his words as he took his punches: straight and clean.

So, after explaining the assignment to Gage in general terms and leaving out a few of the more specific details—no need to put too many cards on the table at once, an act that the exceedingly closed-mouth Gage completely appreciated—Dylan told him to sit tight and wait for his next call. In all likelihood, he told Gage as he ended his call, the plan would get underway by the end of next week. Gage, however, would be on the payroll starting immediately.

Gage had grunted his approval.

Dylan's second phone call was the one he was secretly dreading. He knew he wasn't going to hang up until he got a confirmation, but getting one was going to be far from easy. There would be a great deal of animosity to cut through. Doing so was going to take patience and time. Neither of which he had in any great supply, especially now.

But, schooling himself to keep both his temper and his natural good humor, he pressed the familiar, though seldom used number.

The phone on the other end rang several

times before he finally heard the receiver being picked up.

"Yeah?"

The abrupt greetingless response didn't surprise him. "Cheerful as ever, I see."

"Dylan." It wasn't a question but an assumption. Though months could go by without any contact between them, there was no mistaking each other's voices.

There was no point in building up to this, Dylan thought. He was going to cut right to the heart of the matter. Undoubtedly, even though his twin brother was up in Montana running the ranch they both owned, Cole wasn't so isolated that he didn't know what was happening with their father.

Here goes nothing.

"Once I get a few things squared away, I'm sending Dad up to the ranch. Most likely by the end of next week." He figured giving Cole up to fourteen days to prepare for this was all the time he could afford.

There was silence on the other end. It went on too long.

"Did you hear me?" Dylan finally asked.

"I heard you," Cole replied in his deep, un-hurried voice that so often sounded deceptively disinterested. "You have another ranch some-where?" his twin asked. "Because you sure as hell are *not* sending the old man here to my ranch."

Dylan didn't have the time or the energy to argue. But he didn't particularly want to have to pound this into Cole's head, either. "The ranch is half mine," he reminded his brother.

Cole snorted. "Good. You can put him in your half of the barn." He made it sound as if he was washing his hands of both of them.

Dylan wasn't about to be dismissed, inten-tionally or unintentionally. "Cole, the man's in trouble."

"Yeah, I saw. He's splashed all over the front page of the paper."

Sometime during the drive home, Dylan had become convinced that whatever was going on with their father, it wasn't just about the mistresses and the supposedly missing campaign funds. There was more to it than that. He had the really strong premonition that someone was after their father—and it wasn't just to shoot the breeze. They needed to tuck the senator away somewhere where access was limited.

In the meantime, he needed to get to work on the investigation. The police department, he was willing to bet, really had nothing to work with.

"No," Dylan interrupted, "it goes a lot deeper than that."

Inadvertently, he'd managed to stir his brother's curiosity. "How deep?"

"Deep enough for me to want to hide the old man somewhere where he can't be harmed."

"You think it's come to that?" Cole wanted to know.

"Yes, I do." He had his brother, he hoped, on the ropes.

Cole sighed, obviously none too happy. "Well, even so, you've got a whole damn country to pick from. You don't need just one small plot of land."

"I need a place where I'll know he's going to be safe."

The conversation seemed to be beginning to bore Cole. "In case you've forgotten, this is a working ranch. I don't have time to babysit the old man."

"I'll be sending up a couple of bodyguards with him. All you have to do is to open up the house. Let them stay up there with you."

"'All,'" Cole echoed, mocking the very word as well as the too-innocent-sounding request.

"What'll you want for an encore? A pound of flesh?"

"An IOU note for the pound'll do." And then the humor left Dylan's voice. "This is serious, Cole. I've never seen the old man like this. He looks afraid."

"Afraid," Cole repeated thoughtfully, trying to understand what was at work here. "As in afraid of losing his lifestyle?"

"No," Dylan contradicted him. "Afraid as in afraid of losing his life."

He could almost hear the frown forming on Cole's face. Forming and going clear down to the bone. The frown would be a twin to the one he'd worn himself when he'd realized that he needed to bring Cole in on this. And most likely, the others as well.

But one step at a time, he counseled himself. One step at a time.

"When did you say he was coming?" Cole asked grudgingly.

"Next week. I knew I could count on you."

"Yeah," Cole said, his voice flat, devoid of emotion. And then he added, "You owe me. Big-time."

"Cole," Dylan reminded him. "Like it or not, he is our father."

"Not that I ever noticed. And for the record," he added, "I choose *not*."

"I'll be in touch next week with the details," Dylan promised, knowing that despite his own personal preferences to the contrary, Cole would come through for him—for them. He'd stake his life on that.

It didn't improve his mood any to know, as the other end of the line went dead, that was *exactly* what he was doing.

Chapter 10

If doubts about his father's Chief Staff Assistant's sincerity and her true intentions had occasion to cross Dylan's mind, they quickly disappeared over the course of the next three days. After tying up several loose ends and prevailing upon a couple of associates at the law firm to take over his clients for the next couple of weeks or so, Dylan buckled down to devoting himself completely to the old man's case.

Cindy, as it turned out, proved to be invaluable and, for a woman who had every right to beg off due to her condition, she was also tireless. Even if she did yawn a great deal. Each day she vetoed every suggestion on his part that she call it a day early.

It got to the point that he doubted whether she slept much at all. Except for the first day, when he picked her up, she was at the office each morning when he arrived and remained there during the course of the day, advising him about various files, supplying him with the names of people and businesses that the senator had dealings with; for all intents and purposes, she became his safari guide in this jungle that some referred to as the world of national politics.

She seemed to have it all at her fingertips.

"How did you get so knowledgeable?" Dylan couldn't help asking late one evening. Weary, he paused, closing the file he had been reading.

The office was empty except for the two of them, and the hour, ten o'clock, had nothing to do with it. The moment it had become apparent that the senator had gone into hiding, the people who made up his office staff had pragmatically begun the search for other positions.

Cover your back was a mantra that more than one office staffer embraced.

Times were tough and being associated with a senator who had fallen so scandalously from favor could only be seen as a bad thing. From what he'd heard, his father's staff had almost trampled each other in their hurry to flee.

So why hadn't Cindy fled with the rest of them? he wondered, looking at her across the antique desk his father had bought during his very first term as senator.

And why, looking the way she did, had the young woman voluntarily walked into this snake pit in the first place? She had the kind of face and form that models actively strove for. Killed for. But while a gorgeous face looked wonderful on the cover of a magazine, Dylan knew that in the arena of politics, her looks could ultimately just work against her.

The simple truth of it was, there was still a prejudice against a beautiful woman. The feeling was that if she had looks, then she couldn't possibly have the kind of brains it took to deal with complex, delicate situations.

Cindy looked up and saw Dylan looking at her. It took her a moment to pull her mind back from the file she'd been going through and replay his question. Ordinarily, his questions all revolved around either a file or a meeting between the senator and someone he'd dealt with—supposedly on a professional level. Dylan was still pursuing the idea that the scandal had been leaked by someone who had something to gain from the senator's ignoble fall from grace.

Dylan hadn't asked a personal question— other than what she wanted for lunch when he was placing a delivery order over the phone—since they had begun this investigative marathon.

She turned his question—how had she become so knowledgeable?—over in her mind and shrugged. To her, she was still woefully underinformed. "I keep my ears opened—and I did a lot of reading. Still do." In her opinion, she had a lifetime of reading ahead of her just to keep up.

"Why?" he challenged. Then, before she could say something, he told her, "You should be out, enjoying yourself. Enjoying life," he pointed out. "Not locking yourself up with dry reading matter."

She took a tiny part of that and twisted it around to her advantage.

"How do you know I don't do my reading under some shady oak tree?" she countered with a smile. "Getting fresh air and a hit for my brain cells," she concluded. "And if your next question is why am I here, the answer's easy. It's because I want to make a difference. Life isn't some endless frat party, it's responsibilities heaped on top of more responsibilities. Nobody gets a free pass." That was something she firmly believed. "One way or another, we all wind up paying."

She was thinking of the baby, Dylan guessed. If she was so dead-set against it, if she was doing what she could to remain in denial about her condition, then what was she going to do about it when it grew more demanding? The time in which denial stood her in good stead was growing shorter by the day.

Was she thinking of giving the baby up for adoption? Had she looked into some agency, or was she considering a private adoption?

Questions burned on his tongue, but he knew he had no right to ask. His father was his problem, not Cindy's situation.

Still, he couldn't help thinking that Cindy Jensen was a bit of an enigma. A complex woman. There was nothing straightforward about her, despite that sweet, innocent-look-ing face.

"Everyone else associated with this cam-paign, this office, is scrambling to find other work with another senator or congressman. As far as the senator's career goes, they're con-vinced that the fat lady has sung. So why are you still here?" he asked again.

He wanted to know what made her tick, what motivated her. It had been a long time since he'd felt this amount of curiosity about a woman. But, he was beginning to realize, Cindy Jensen was no ordinary woman. She was an intriguing dynamo.

"Maybe I'm just tone-deaf," she suggested, keeping a straight face. "Or maybe it's not the fat lady they heard but just some coyote howling at the moon. In the immortal words of Yogi Berra," she began, reaching for her all-time favorite quote, words she chose to live by,

"'It ain't over 'til it's over.' And I don't think it's over," she tacked on in case he missed her meaning.

She'd always loved that line. It was what she had clung to whenever she felt in danger of being down-and-out. That wasn't hard, seeing as how she was a single, abused, mother-to-be of a child she had no desire to hold. A child whose life, a life she was, even now, terrified of messing up, had been conceived in violence.

"What do you hope to get out of this?" Dylan asked her.

"'Get out of this?'" she echoed. Why would he ask something like that? "I hope to get the senator out of this—help bail him out and get him back on his feet again so he can go back to dealing with the public and making his contribution."

Dylan leaned back, listening to her speak. The people he worked with were self-absorbed, one worse that the other. It was nice being away from that. Even if it was only for a little while. She was a breath of fresh air—if she was on the level.

"And that's enough?" he questioned.

"It is for me," she assured him. "Look, you don't seem to like your father very much," she observed. "But I do." She saw the glimmer of suspicion in his eyes again and immediately set him straight. "No, not in *that* way. I respect him a great deal. I think he's done a lot of good for his constituents and I think that, despite opinions to the contrary, he still has a lot to give.

"And I think you're right," she went on. "I think that someone is out to destroy the senator. I don't know why, I just know that if there's anything, anything at all, that I can do to prevent that, then I'm ready to jump in and come to his rescue."

Dylan sat mystified, listening to her. If she

was acting, then she deserved an Academy Award right here, right now.

"My father's lucky to have you," Dylan told her.

That wasn't the way she saw it. "I was lucky to have him," she countered. Since her statement probably stirred up more questions than it put to rest, she decided to tell him just a little more of the reason she was so loyal to his father, building on what she'd mentioned to him the other day.

"When my marriage was falling apart, it was your father who stepped in and gave me someone to lean on." This was hard for her, but she was the one who had started it. To end it abruptly wouldn't have been right. "I don't have a family. Your father provided me with the kind of emotional support that I needed in order to send my ex packing."

"No family," Dylan repeated. "Your parents weren't around?" He knew he was pushing her, but this small opening might be the only opportunity he'd get to ask her questions.

He saw her flush and realized he'd overstepped his boundary. He was about to apologize when Cindy answered his question. "My mother died when I was around four."

"And your father?"

Her shoulders rose and then fell in a vague, careless shrug. "Might be dead. Might still be alive. I really don't know. He deposited me at a local fire station, gave me a five-dollar bill to clutch in my hand and took off. I was four at the time. The firemen turned me over to social services. That was the only life I knew until I turned eighteen."

There was only one conclusion to be drawn from her statement. But even as he said it, he couldn't fathom turning his back on the sad-eyed little girl she must have been.

"You weren't adopted?"

"No. But that was because, technically, I

wasn't an orphan. My father hadn't written away his 'rights' to me. He could still come back and claim me—not that he would have. To avoid any of the legal hassles that might crop up for the agency I was never in the running for adoptive parents."

He couldn't imagine what that had been like. Being alone like that. Granted he'd had a no-show father, but his mother had been there when he was growing up. And his brothers and Lana had always been there for him. That meant a lot.

"No bonding with anyone at any of the foster homes they sent you to?" he asked.

There had been families she'd tried her best to please. Families she tried to make like her. But it was easier just keeping her distance. Less pain that way. Less disappointment.

"This was life, not a Disney movie," she told him.

Was that bitterness he heard in her voice? It

was completely out of character. He couldn't tell and her expression wasn't giving anything away.

More questions began to take root in his mind. He found himself far more interested in her than in his father's situation.

He told himself it was only his natural curiosity directing him, but there was more to it than that and he knew it. The truth was he'd been attracted to Cindy from the first moment he saw her and her pouty little mouth. The snippets of her life that she made him privy to just seemed to increase that attraction, despite efforts on his part to the contrary.

"Was your ex part of the system when he was growing up?" he asked. The words sounded stilted to his ear. Where was the silver-tongued lawyer hiding these days? He could stand channeling him because, right now, he sounded like some freshman law student, incapable of forming a proper sentence. He half expected her to tell him to take a flying leap.

Instead, she answered his intrusive question.

"No. I met him at a community college. He was in one of my classes, I forget which one," she confessed. "What I do remember was thinking that he was everything I thought I wanted—good-looking, charming, sweet, interested in me," she added with a soft smile. "And kind. Very kind. That was the most important trait of all for me." Her smile faded. "Turns out that was the biggest lie about him."

She sighed, continuing. "Either that, or there was something about me that turned him from a kind, sweet man to a jealous, raving lunatic. He bought me a cell phone and then ruined the gift by calling me all the time, asking me where I was at that second. It was his way of trying to control my every movement. Of keeping tabs on me. He thought he owned me."

It sounded like a really rotten existence. "Why didn't you just leave him?"

"The day I said I was going to leave him, he grabbed my throat, shoved me hard against the wall and shouted into my face, telling me that if I even so much as *thought* about leaving him, he'd slit my throat from ear to ear, ensuring that I wouldn't be going anywhere, ever."

Even as she recited the details, she couldn't help shivering. The threat, made many months ago, still rattled her.

Dylan could feel himself getting steadily more and more angry. Bullies had always brought out the fury in him. He hated anyone who thought they had a right to throw their weight around, intimidating someone weaker, smaller than they were. Bullies *never* picked on anyone their own size.

"Why didn't you go to the police?" he wanted to know. As far as he saw it, it would have been a simple enough manner.

"With what?" she countered. "I had no proof. It would be a matter of he-said, she-said. And everyone thought he was such a great guy. I was the only one who got to see that awful side of him.

"I knew that if I pointed that out, they'd think it was all in my head and tell me to get counseling. The whole situation, the fear, the controlling, the mind games, they all gave Dean this sense of power over me."

Her voice grew distant as she tried to push the horror she'd lived through away from her, tried to pretend that it had happened to someone else instead of to her.

"He told me that everything would be all right if I just went along with whatever he said. I tried," she confessed. "I really did. But that just doesn't work when you're dealing with someone who's completely irrational."

She took a breath before continuing. "In Dean's mind, I could do no right. If I talked to another man, I wasn't just talking, I had to be propositioning him. So he beat me as if I had slept with the guy."

How could she have stood for it? Dylan couldn't help wondering. She seemed so independent now, it was hard to see her in that other light. "You were working for my father by then?"

She nodded. "And Dean didn't like it. He kept pressuring me to quit. When I refused, he retaliated the only way he knew how." She raised her eyes to his. "With his fists."

"He hit you," Dylan said incredulously. He knew that was what she was saying, but he still couldn't begin to fathom that kind of a coward.

She nodded. "Always in strategic places. Places he knew I wouldn't show anyone, despite the fact that he kept calling me a slut and a—well, never mind what the other names were. You get the idea."

He more than got it, Dylan thought angrily. "So when did my father get involved?"

"The day Dean slipped and left a mark on me that couldn't be covered up with clothes." That had been the day, she thought, that she had actually been reborn, although it hadn't felt that way at the time. "Even makeup wouldn't do it. I couldn't cover up the shiner enough to make it disappear."

She remembered it as if it had happened yesterday. "Your father took me aside and talked to me. He didn't believe I had walked into a door the way I told him. I had a restraining order against Dean in my hands by the end of the day, a place to stay and a divorce in the works in twenty-four hours. The senator did all that for me because he said he wanted me to be safe." Her eyes shifted to Dylan's face. She could almost see what he was thinking. "And in case you're wondering, yes, I was suspicious of his motives. I kept waiting for the senator to 'collect his reward' for being so helpful.

"But he never did," she said proudly. "Never tried so much as to touch me. He was actually just concerned about my safety. *That's* why I'm here, helping you help him. Because if the senator *hadn't* helped me, who knows if I'd even be alive today? They say that, left unchecked, domestic violence only escalates," she told him quietly. "In Dean's case, that meant it likely would have led to murder by now."

He nodded, tactfully refraining from commenting. It was enough that she was aware of what could have happened to her. He wondered if this was as over as she apparently thought it was. Something told him it wouldn't truly be over until the man was in prison. "Where's your ex now?"

She shook her head. "I don't know." Moreover, she didn't want to know. She just hoped she'd never have to see him again. "The last thing he said to me was that he was going to get even with me for humiliating him the way I had, even if it took him a lifetime."

That explained pretty clearly why she was so jumpy, Dylan thought. It didn't take a genius or a psychic to figure out that she was afraid that her ex was going to make good on his promise.

Apparently his father wasn't the only one who could do with having a bodyguard around.

"And you haven't heard from Dean since?" he asked her.

Cindy shook her head, suddenly feeling very weary. "I think he's afraid that the senator was going to do something to him, legally or otherwise. They had a confrontation when Dean came to the office that last time. Dean threatened to drag me home to 'talk' to me. The senator overheard Dean and informed him that he wasn't to bother me. Not only that, but if he ever saw him near me again, he was going to make Dean's life a living hell." She stopped, her eyes widening as a thought dawned on her. "You don't think Dean's behind this scandal hitting the media, do you?"

This Dean character didn't sound as if he was capable of any involved plotting. "Does he have a way of accessing that kind of information?" Dylan asked her. Cindy shook her head. "Then no, he's probably just a lot of hot air. Remember, a bully is someone who depends on fear doing his work for him."

She flushed, realizing that she'd just wasted precious time talking about herself—Dylan had stopped working to listen to her. "How did we get started on this topic, anyway?"

"I asked you a question," he told her, then went on to say, "I needed to know about you."

The confession both warmed her and made her extremely nervous. She felt as if some of her safeguards had just crumbled. "Why?"

"Because you seem to see the good in my father and I wanted to know what it was that you saw and what made you stick by him in the first place," he told her honestly. "You didn't strike me as a gold digger."

She was sure Dean would have had another, far more derogatory term for it.

"That's nice," she replied dryly.

He hadn't intended to offend her. "It was meant as a compliment," he pointed out. "You not being one." God, next he was going to drop his articles and his pronouns. What was the matter with him?

"And I took it as such," she answered. Then, to prove her point she asked, "You can still walk, right?" There was a smile glimmering in her eyes as she asked.

An isolated lyric from an old song buried deep within his childhood, left there courtesy of an Irish nanny, flashed through Dylan's mind—"When Irish eyes are smiling." The point of it was, he finally understood what "smiling eyes" were.

"C'mon, it's late," he said, pushing away from the desk and standing up. "Let's call it a night and I'll buy you dinner."

She *was* getting tired, she thought. Maybe it was time to go home. Raising her gaze to his, she said, "I'm not hungry."

He wasn't about to get turned down that easily. "All right, I'll buy you a cup of tea and you can watch me have dinner."

Everything she'd ever been through told her to turn him down and say no. But there still remained within her a tiny kernel of the optimist that she longed to be. And, looking back later, she realized that it was that kernel that was ultimately responsible for her saying, "All right."

Chapter 11

The name of the restaurant he took her to, Gallagher's, suggested an old-fashioned pub that focused on alcoholic beverages rather than on the food that they served, but the establishment prided itself on what they referred to as "home cooking" and it was—if home happened to come along with a resident chef who knew how to bring out the very best in every meal. The portions, rather than minuscule servings artistically arranged on a plate, were of a decent size, designed to satisfy the appetite of a functioning adult rather than of a supermodel watching her waistline. The lighting was subdued and the atmosphere soothing.

All in all, it seemed like the perfect place to come to at the end of a long, hard day.

They were seated almost immediately, ushered to a table for two that had its share of privacy. After leaving them each with a menu, the tall, thin young waiter unobtrusively passed by their table twice. Each time he would glance in their direction, waiting for the proper cue that they were ready to order.

After a couple of minutes, Cindy opened her menu and began to scan the pages inside. Tempting photos went along with descriptions of the various meals that were offered, and they stirred her dormant appetite. "I guess maybe I will have something to eat after all."

Dylan looked up at her, pleased that she'd decided to join him. "Appetite finally kicked in, I take it?"

There was a little of that, but that wasn't her

main reason for deciding to order something more substantial than just tea. "It's more that I just don't want to have the waiter continuing to look at me funny."

Dylan looked around for their waiter, but the blond food server, who looked barely old enough to shave, wasn't watching them. He was taking another table's order.

"He's not looking at you funny," Dylan assured her, turning back to his menu. "He's admiring you and being jealous of me."

That came out so smoothly, she almost believed him. Except that she knew better. It was just a line. "Why would he be jealous?"

"Because he thinks you're with me. And, technically speaking, you are, but not the way he thinks. Not the way it counts," Dylan added, raising his eyes to hers.

His gaze was so deep, so penetrating, Cindy felt her breath catch in her throat. She told herself not to be stupid.

Her mouth curved just the smallest bit. "I guess your father's ability to be charming and smooth talk his way into things did get passed on after all."

At any other time, Dylan might have taken that as an insult. But he knew she didn't mean it that way. "One big difference."

"Oh?" Cindy closed the menu, giving Dylan her undivided attention, even as she had to tell herself that her pulse wasn't actually launching into double time. "And that is?"

"Sincerity." Dylan never blinked an eye. "My father's smooth talk is second nature to him. He's used it as a tool to charm his way into the sort of lucrative situations that most people only dream about."

She wasn't about to be snowed. Or distracted. "And you? You don't 'smooth talk' your way into things that are to your advantage?"

Very slowly he shook his head. "I don't smooth talk at all. That's where the sincerity part comes in," he told her, the smile on his lips sneaking its way under her skin. Pulling her in despite her firm desire to resist.

"You're sincere," she said, her tone telling him exactly what a crock she thought that was. "Every word out of your mouth is sincere." It wasn't a statement, it was a challenge. She was daring him to say yes.

Dylan leaned in, his eyes holding her completely captive even though she was putting up what she would have considered to be one damn good fight.

"Yes," he replied. "Especially just now."

No, don't believe him, Cindy. You know better. It's all just empty talk.

Her heart increased its tempo, now beating in triple time. Cindy broke eye contact with him. She took the deep-green linen napkin from the table and pretended to be engrossed in watching her hands as she carefully unfolded it and spread it out on her lap.

"I've been here before, Dylan," she informed him quietly.

The seemingly sharp change in conversational direction caught him up short for a moment. "You mean to this restaurant?"

"No." She'd made a fatal mistake, she realized the second the words had come out of her mouth. She really didn't want to talk about her failed marriage. Cindy raised her eyes to his again. "No," she repeated. "To this line of conversation. To this sort of subtle deception."

His hands tightened on the menu he was still holding. It was the only outward sign of his ire. "Meaning your husband."

Raising her chin defensively came instinctively to her. "You probably think I have to be some kind of village idiot to have been taken in by Dean. To have believed him when, after each incident, he said he would change." And maybe she was, she thought, struggling not to think of herself in those terms. "At his best,

Dean was charming, kind, sweet. In short, everything any woman could have possibly wished for. It was only after we were married that he started to let his mask down."

Is that what she thought? That he was judging her? Not having walked in her shoes, he had no right to do anything like that.

He almost reached for her hand in a show of comfort, but somehow knew she'd only withdraw into herself if he did that. So he kept his hand where it was.

"No, I don't think you're a village idiot. A lot of people are taken in by people like that. Taken in because they can't begin to imagine lying to someone. They don't understand why someone would go to such lengths to lie to them and then go back on their word and mistreat them all over again."

Dylan saw the surprised look in her eyes. "See, I do understand," he told her, his voice low, soothing. "The reason I think you might be just slightly lacking in mental acuity is that you don't see the difference."

"The difference?" she asked, not following his meaning.

He nodded. "Between someone like that miserable excuse for a human being and me."

"Because you're so sincere," Cindy said, repeating his claim. There was a touch of mockery in her voice. She was still afraid to let her guard down, even a little.

If he wasn't completely honest with her, he was never going to get her to trust him. *Here goes everything,* he thought.

"Look, I feel that there's something going on between us, something more than just both of us being interested in saving my father's hide. Something intense," he emphasized. "And as intense as I think it is—as intense as it is to me—I want you to know that I'm never going to do anything you don't want me to do. Simply put, if anything's to happen between us, you're going to have to give me the green light here."

She stared at him. Did he really think she was that simple minded?

"And if I don't?" she challenged. "If, let's say, we're at my door and you're kissing me good-night. *Really* kissing me good-night. Things look as if they're about to get hot and heavy and then, to use your metaphor, I suddenly have second thoughts and turn on the red light—" Her voice trailed off, waiting for him to complete the statement.

"Then I stop."

Yeah, right, she thought sarcastically. "You stop," she said out loud, completely unconvinced. "Just like that?"

A self-deprecating smile curved his lips. "Well, no, not just like that. I'll probably have to take a hell of a long, cold shower." His eyes touched hers. "But, yes, I stop." He could see that she still didn't quite believe him. Dylan sighed, shaking his head. "Cindy, you need to wrap your head around the fact that I will never hurt you."

She found herself wanting to believe him. Really wanting to believe that there were men out there who *weren't* like her ex. Decent men who didn't turn into sadistic monsters once they had worn her down.

But she could only work with what she knew. "You say that now," she began.

Dylan cut in. "I *mean* that now," he told her quietly, firmly. "And I'll mean it later. Cindy, you really need to believe that your worthless ex-husband was the exception, not the rule. Most guys are not like him."

The waiter returned just then, preventing any immediate, further exchange. "Have you made up your minds yet?" he asked politely.

"Yes," Cindy replied. Her eyes met Dylan's fleetingly, then she lowered them to look down at the menu. "I have."

Dylan felt an unexpected surge go through him. For reasons he couldn't begin to explain, he suddenly felt as excited, as nervous as a teenager.

More, actually, he reflected, since he'd never really gone through these kinds of feelings when he was that age. Pursued by girls for most of his life, he'd entered the world of manhood and sex fairly confidently, with an assurance that kept him in good stead.

This was something completely different.

He felt the urge to tell the waiter that they were going to get their dinners to go, but he forced himself to refrain, to behave as if there was nothing different about this dinner than any of the others he'd had over the years. That there was nothing different about this particular dining partner that set her apart from any of the others.

But in his gut, he sensed that there was.

This one is going to count, he told himself.

The next moment, Dylan cautioned himself to proceed slowly, for his own sake, not just for hers.

Because Dylan wanted to maintain an absolutely clear head, he skipped his customary glass of wine with dinner. It ordinarily took a great many more than one glass for him to feel the effects of alcohol, but he was taking no chances. He also didn't want Cindy thinking, if something *did* take place tonight, that it was happening in part because of the alcohol.

Besides, just looking at her right now was intoxicating enough. He didn't need any wine.

Dinner seemed to take forever, but oddly enough, Dylan didn't really mind. He'd expected impatience to tug demandingly on his nerve endings. Instead, he caught himself enjoying the whole experience, enjoying just talking to Cindy.

It was a little like watching a rare flower

opening up, tilting its head toward the sun, its petals being ruffled by an early-morning spring breeze.

Damn, he was waxing poetic. This *was* a different experience from those he normally had. She definitely brought out a different side to him, he mused.

"Will there be anything else?" the waiter asked as a swiftly moving busboy cleared away their empty dinner plates. "Dessert, perhaps?" The young man looked from Dylan to Cindy, looking for a taker. "We have an excellent selection."

Dylan raised a quizzical eyebrow in her direction. Why that struck her as incredibly sexy she wasn't sure, but it did, and she was amazed that she could actually still form words. Inside, she was vibrating like a tuning fork. A tuning fork with an incredibly dry mouth.

"No, nothing else, thank you," she told the

waiter. "If I eat another bite, I'm going to have to be rolled out to the car."

Dylan grinned as the image she suggested flashed through his mind. "I can think of worse things," he told her.

The remark caused the pragmatic waiter to look back at her, giving her the option to change her mind. But she shook her head. She'd meant what she'd said. She was full almost to the point of bursting. Dinner for her normally involved something light and small. What she'd just consumed was way more than she was used to eating at this time of the evening.

"We could get a dessert to go," Dylan suggested. "You might want to have it later."

"No, really. I'll explode," she told him. "Maybe next time."

The words were out of her mouth before she could stop to think them through. Cindy flushed, embarrassed. Now he was going to think that she assumed he was going to do this again.

She bit her lower lip, raised her eyes to his and said, "I didn't mean—"

Dylan cut her off. He didn't want to hear an apology, especially since he wasn't ruling out the possibility of what she'd inadvertently said. The idea of taking her out again appealed to him, no matter how tonight ultimately turned out.

"Next time it is," he told her, then nodded at the waiter. "I think we're finished here. Bring me the bill, please."

The waiter didn't have to be told twice. Disappearing, he was back in less than five minutes with the bill. As he placed it in front of Dylan, Cindy took out her wallet.

"What are you doing?" he asked as he reached into his inside pocket for his own wallet.

"Paying my share."

Dylan frowned. This time, he did reach across the table and put his hand on hers. But the intent was to stop her, not to offer comfort. "No, you're not. I distinctly remember asking you out to dinner."

"No, you didn't. You asked me if I was hungry," she recalled.

"Same thing."

She tried to take out several bills. "Not really."

He pulled the small silver tray with its bill closer to his side of the table. "You are the stubbornest woman I've ever dealt with. Let me pay this if for no other reason than I have more money than you do."

"That shouldn't matter," she pointed out.

"Humor me," he told her.

With a sigh, she withdrew her hand and the money. "Okay, consider yourself humored."

Amusement played on his lips. She was definitely a one-of-a-kind woman. "Thank you."

Leaving far more than the amount on the bill, Dylan rose from the table intending to help her with her chair. But she had already risen to her feet. "Anyone ever tell you that you make it damn hard to play the gentleman?"

"You can blame that on my upbringing. Where I grew up, if you weren't first in line, you did without. It's a hard habit to break," she admitted.

"We'll practice," he told her. This time, when he placed his hand to her back, she only stiffened marginally. And then relaxed.

Progress, he thought.

They walked out of Gallagher's and discovered that the heat had all but disappeared into the velvet darkness that wrapped itself around them like a familiar soft black stole.

"Do you eat like that all the time?" she wanted to know.

He thought for a moment. "Not all the time, but pretty much," he had to admit.

She did a quick survey of his physique, as if to assure herself that she wasn't mistaken. Nope, she wasn't. The man had an exceedingly trim body, not to mention that it looked athletic. "It's a wonder you're not twice your size."

He grinned. "It'd be too expensive, not to mention time-consuming, to get all brand-new suits." He winked at her as he stopped to unlock his car doors. "It's a matter of exercising a little willpower versus a lot of inconvenience."

She got in on her side and gave him her address in case it had slipped his mind. It hadn't.

They drove in silence for a few minutes until the silence grew too large to contain in the car.

At the next red light he stopped and looked at her. "Tired?" he asked.

She was too wired at the moment to know the answer to that. She supposed once that component was taken away, she more than likely would just collapse. But for now, she was far too wired to be tired.

"Just thinking," she replied.

"About what?" Dylan asked, then thought better of it. He didn't want to risk getting into a heated discussion about boundaries, so he set the record straight right at the outset. "If it's private, you don't have to answer me."

"It's not private," she assured him. "I was just thinking about how good the dinner was…"

It was only partially the truth. Her thoughts had only fleetingly touched upon the simple excellence of the meal she'd had tonight. For the most part, her thoughts were revolving around what had yet to happen.

If it was going to happen, she amended.

She was taking a great deal for granted here. And she honestly didn't know whether she'd be happier if it *did* happen or if he just took her to her door and left her there.

You do too know, an annoying little voice in her head whispered. *You want him to come in. You want him to stay the night. You want* him.

Cindy did what she could to block the voice and look as if nothing out of the ordinary was going on in her head.

"Yeah, me too," he replied.

It took her a second to realize what he was commenting on. She was going to have to get her head under control, she told herself. With that, she looked at Dylan doubtfully. He was thinking about the food at dinner? "Really?"

The smile on his lips were infectious. "I am if you are," he replied.

She laughed and some of the tension that insisted on dancing through her body began to abate. "You make it sound like a two-for-one sale."

Why, if he'd had no wine at all, did she look prettier to him now than she had earlier? Not just prettier but more sensual as well. He could feel desire spreading out within him like a panther stretching after a nap.

"Something like that," he murmured.

Her cell phone rang, intruding into the moment. "Maybe it's the senator," Cindy said as she dug into her purse. Finding the phone, she opened it and pressed it to her ear. "Hello?" There was an indistinguishable noise on the other end and the sound of someone breathing. "Hello? Is someone there?"

"Who is it?" Dylan asked.

She shook her head in response. "Hello?" she said, raising her voice despite the fact that she didn't hear any static on the other end. Why weren't they saying anything? And then there was the sound of someone hanging up. Dead air met her ear. Cindy looked at her cell phone's screen. The caller ID was no help. The number was blocked. "They hung up," she murmured

"Bad connection or wrong number," he guessed.

"Yeah." The way she said it, Dylan had a feeling she didn't think so.

Was someone playing mind games with them?

"You know, sometimes a wrong number is just that," he reminded her.

She flashed him a smile that was a little uneasy around the edges. "You're right," she agreed. She was being silly, she told herself. And jumpy.

But then, maybe Dylan had something to do with that, she thought, slanting a glance in his direction as a ribbon of anticipation wove through her.

They were approaching the underground parking structure beneath her high-rise apartment building. Rather than briefly park at the building's entrance and let her get out, Dylan, without hesitation, drove straight into the structure. Once inside, he followed the labyrinthine path. Above it, like bright Christmas decorations out of season, neon-red arrows all pointed in the direction of more parking.

Heat began pricking at Cindy's skin, increasing further as Dylan drove his car in to the structure.

"What are you doing?" she asked, the words all but sticking to the roof of her dry mouth.

"Looking for parking so that I can take you up to your apartment." He would have thought that was pretty self-evident. "It's the only decent thing to do," he added.

"And you're a great believer in doing the decent thing?" Was that her being coy? Flirting? Or what she felt passed for flirting, she amended silently. What was going on here?

She was both nervous and excited, even as she warned herself not to be.

"Whenever possible," he replied to her mocking question. He stole a glance at her now that they were relatively alone and unthreatened by traffic. "Whenever possible," he repeated.

Instead of feeling a sense of relief at his profession of honorability, her nerves instantly spiked even higher than before, fed by an anticipation the magnitude of which she had never encountered before.

Just what did she think she was anticipating here, Cindy asked herself. Women were a dime a dozen for this man. Why would he bother singling her out?

And why did she so desperately want him to?

Chapter 12

Intellectually, Cindy knew perfectly well that the air-conditioning system in her apartment building was working just fine. The maintenance department prided itself on keeping things not simply running, but running well.

In addition, the air-conditioning system in the elevator presently taking them up to her floor was alive and well.

By all rights, she should have felt cool if not utterly comfortable. But she was neither. She felt hot, as if the air around her had suddenly stopped moving and had taken on the properties of the inside of an oven that had been on for a while.

Her quickening pulse might have had something to do with the shift in temperature she could swear she detected.

She was being an idiot, Cindy told herself impatiently. There was no reason to feel like this, no reason to be acutely aware of every molecule of air around her, every step she took.

But she was.

She left the elevator and walked in what felt like slow motion to her apartment door. Dylan was beside her, step for achingly slow step, apparently unaware of the fact that she had her own personal sauna wrapped tightly around her.

Stopping before her door, Cindy squared her shoulders and turned around, an empty smile she didn't feel fixed on her face.

"Thank you," she said to Dylan. "Thank you for dinner and for, well, everything," she concluded with a quick, careless shrug of her slim shoulders.

Dylan inclined his head, an escorting knight taking his leave of the queen. "My pleasure entirely," he assured her.

That was when she realized that if she didn't say anything to stop him, to invite him into her apartment, he was going to leave.

Just as he'd said he would.

Did she want him to? Did she want this to end right here, at her door, or did she want the evening to go further? To have him go further?

And if he did, just how far was further? What kind of boundaries was she going to set?

Was she going to set boundaries?

How was she going to feel, waiting for that other shoe to drop? Waiting for Dylan to turn from the man she wanted him to remain, into—

Her train of thought abruptly stopped moving forward, its journey into darkness halted because Dylan was taking her face between his hands.

The next moment, his lips were on hers. Lightly. Softly. Causing explosions inside her that were in diametric contrast to the gentleness he was displaying.

The sigh she heard escaping was her own.

Afraid that Dylan might still leave despite what he'd just initiated, she threw her arms around his neck and kissed him back with more feeling than she'd thought she was capable of demonstrating after everything Dean had put her through.

The hallway, always well-lit, suddenly began to darken around her until, finally, the light just seemed to completely disappear.

Everything disappeared except for the heat that was being generated in this small piece of space that they were sharing.

Excitement pulsed wildly through her, growing ever bigger, as Cindy surrendered herself to the feeling that was stealing not just her breath but her very mind as well.

The kiss grew until it was far too deep, far too wide for her to find her way back by herself.

Not that she wanted to.

When the all-consuming kiss did finally end, it was Dylan who ended it, Dylan who stepped back, not she. Slowly, the lights seemed to re-enter the scene, and a little of the cloud that had encompassed her brain began to lift.

But her pulse continued hammering wildly.

Her eyes never left his as she held her breath, waiting to see what came next. Praying it was what she wanted.

"I'd like to come in," he told her, amazed that he could feel so very much so soon. What was happening inside him almost defied description and was actually beyond his scope of experience, at least, until now. "But only if you want me to."

He was actually leaving it up to her, she thought. Just as he'd said.

Cindy didn't answer him. Instead, she turned away from Dylan. The next moment, she'd unlocked the door to her apartment and opened it. Wide. The invitation was unspoken but nonetheless clear.

But even as she stepped into her apartment, dropping her purse on the floor, an obstacle to be gotten out of the way, Dylan caught her by the arm and turned her around to face him.

"I meant what I said earlier," he told her, his expression so sincere it almost hurt her to look at him. "I'm never going to do anything you don't want me to."

Never rather than *not.*

It had the sound of the future about it, she thought. Was it just a slip on his part, or was she reading too much into the word?

Or—?

Don't get ahead of yourself, she warned

sternly. *You don't even know if this is the real him yet, or just an act to lull you into complacency.*

If it was the latter, he was in for a hell of a surprise because she'd learned her lesson. She wasn't going to be anyone's rug or anyone's punching bag no matter how bone-melting their kisses were. Somewhere amid filing for divorce, discovering she was pregnant and taking on the senator's fight, she thought proudly, she'd forged a backbone. No one was ever going to crush her self-esteem again.

Cindy searched for some kind of flippant comeback to his words, but when she raised her eyes to his, her mind went completely, numbingly blank. And when her soul stepped forward to take over, she could only murmur, "I know."

The scary part was that she believed it. Believed him. And even as she silently upbraided herself for being so simple, so gullible, a part of her prayed that he wasn't just feeding her a line. That Dylan truly meant what he'd just said.

And then, there was no more time for thought, for weighing things pro and con, not even a second left for hesitation.

Because he was kissing her again.

Kissing her as if the end of the world was waiting for them both just outside her door and this was their very last chance to snatch up a tiny shred of warm happiness.

The light gray carpeted floor from her door to her bedroom became littered with clothing haphazardly cast off by eager fingers, tossed away without regard in the wake of a vast, bottomless hunger that was eating away at both of them.

A hunger to discover all the secret places that only two lovers could know about one another.

The moment they crossed the threshold into her apartment, they went from two separate people working for a common goal to two would-be lovers longing to fuse into one.

Cindy's scope of experience was woefully lacking. Before Dean there had been a boy in high school who had painfully fumbled away her virginity, leaving her more frustrated and embarrassed than fulfilled. Dean had been a good lover, at least the first few times they had been together. But soon afterward, his touch only made her cringe and there was absolutely no joy, no heart-pounding anticipation associated with what happened between them in the bedroom. There were only episodes of sex, of couplings she forced herself to endure, silently counting the minutes until the experience was over.

What was happening now between her and Dylan made her realize what lovemaking could be like, what it *should* be like, if the two people involved were right for each other. And this felt oh so right.

His touch was tender, as if he was first tentatively exploring regions to ascertain whether or not it was all right for him to continue. Once he was sure, he turned it up a notch, and then two, and then three and more until she was utterly certain that she was going to go up in flames and was more than happy about it.

Desire raged through her, bringing with it an eagerness completely unfamiliar to her. A wild eagerness she discovered herself savoring and rejoicing over.

Damn, but she was a revelation. He hadn't expected the petite woman to be so in tune with his every movement, so receptive to his every touch. Hadn't expected to react to her at this intense a level.

Each curve he caressed only made him want to caress her even more. The tiny sounds she made as he familiarized himself with the feel of her, the very taste of her skin, enflamed him and made him more eager to touch her, to kiss her, to explore every inch along her body, discover every secret it was demurely keeping.

Each pass had his heart actually pounding faster. He was in awe of her and of his powerful reaction to her. By evening's end, he wanted to know her body better than he knew his own.

And then, as he wandered through this brand-new frontier, she caught him by surprise. Instead of lying there, sweetly, almost innocently, receptive, Cindy reached for him. And then she began to feather her long, delicate fingers along his sides, his back, his hips, mimicking his movements and yet making every single one of them her own. Overwhelming desire hardened him with the speed of light.

As she touched, stroked, smiled, Cindy managed to steal his breath away and brought him to the brink so quickly, he had to exercise extreme control at the last moment in order to be able to prolong this experience between them.

It was far from easy. Looking back, he was

convinced that it was probably the most diffi-cult thing he had ever undertaken, but some-how, he succeeded in holding back a little longer.

Long enough to prime her and bring her to the explosive flowering of her first climax with just the right pressure of his tongue along her ultra-sensitive skin.

As she cried out, he saw her eyes widen, saw the stunned look of surprise on her face and made the correct assumption. She might not have been a virgin, but this, he was fairly sure, was her very first time for a complete experience.

Empowered, his own willpower hanging on by a shredded thread, Dylan laced his fingers through hers, positioned himself over Cindy's damp, eager body and with one swift move-ment, entered her.

In precisely one second he had sealed their two bodies, making them one.

And then Dylan began to move, at first slowly, then more quickly, choosing a tempo that he could only hope would coax Cindy up to her second crest of all-encompassing satisfaction.

Pacing himself as best he could, Dylan still found himself racing with Cindy to capture the adrenaline-pumping, elusive prize.

Her spontaneous cry against his lips, the way she arched hard into him at the very last moment, told him that he had succeeded even as his own ability to think was temporarily wiped away. He became caught up in the grip of consuming ecstasy.

And when it happened, surging, powerful and meteoric, he didn't want to let the sensation go.

But there was no choice in the matter and slowly, despite efforts to the contrary, he began the descent back to reality and Cindy's more than slightly rumpled queen-size bed.

As consciousness of his surroundings gradually began to seep in, he realized he was still holding Cindy tightly to him. Still experiencing a degree of tenderness toward her that was remarkably new for him.

He continued to hold her to him a moment longer, then eased himself back. What he did next was also out of character for him. Shifting his weight from her, Dylan remained on the bed rather than getting up and getting dressed. He felt no hurry to leave, no desire to separate himself from what had just happened. Instead, he tucked Cindy against him as if that would somehow prolong the experience they'd just shared.

This protective feeling was something new, something unusual. Explanations and justifications to himself were for later, he decided, when his brain was once again up and running at its maximum capacity. Right now, he had to admit, only a small portion of his brain was functioning at all.

Dylan took in a deep breath and then let it out slowly, centering himself.

Going with instincts rather than bothering to mentally sort things out and waiting until he was in full mental control, he kissed the top of Cindy's head and murmured, "You are full of surprises, Chief Staff Assistant Jensen."

Euphoria was still wrapped around her, but its grip was loosening. Was this what it was supposed to be like? she wondered. Was making love with a man supposed to feel like a thousand New Year's Eve celebrations all rolled up into one? And that absolutely wondrous explosion—for lack of a better word—how was it that she had managed to miss experiencing that over these last few years? Was it because Dean had devolved into a narcissistic, inept lover, in effect, emotionally and physically raping her the last time they were together? Or was there some other explanation for having missed out on this gratifying last step all this time?

Now she realized what all the noise had been about, why people put themselves out time after time. They were all desperately searching for what she had just experienced for the very first time.

Thanks to Dylan.

Despite all precautions, she felt her heart warming toward him.

The teasing tone he'd taken with her faded, moved aside by a sliver of concern. Cindy wasn't talking. Had he hurt her? Frightened her? Done something, despite his best efforts, to upset her? Why wasn't she responding to his playful wonder at her abilities to arouse him so fully?

"Cindy? Are you all right?" he asked. He raised him-self up on his elbow to look at her face. "Say something. Are you all right?" he repeated.

"No," she answered quietly. "I'm not all right." And then the flash of teeth as she grinned gave her away. "I'm terrific. Absolutely, wondrously terrific."

Stretching against him like a seductive, sensual feline, Cindy turned her body toward his as she stretched again. Crucial sections brushed against one another, stirring him.

Stirring her.

"Was that what it's supposed to be like? That wild, wild feeling inside, is that—?" Her voice trailed off as she waited for him to fill in the blank.

With a delighted laugh—something he realized he hadn't been capable for a while now—Dylan brushed the tip of his thumb along her lower lip and discovered that the very act excited him.

"Just a preview of things to come," he promised, completing her sentence.

"A preview?" she echoed quizzically.

"Yes." His smile slipped under her skin and curled itself into her belly. "Here, let me show you," he proposed.

It was the last word that was exchanged between them for quite a while as he set about giving her an encore performance, taking them both back to the brink of ecstasy and beyond.

Allowing them both to forget, if only for a little while, the gravity of the life that existed just beyond their perimeters.

In a room where men checked their names at the door, pretending to maintain an aura of anonymity, a tall, heavyset imposing man sat in a wide, winged chair, frowning at the glass of cognac he held in his hand.

The liquid within the glass shifted ever so slightly, coating the sides of the glass, momentarily leaving a telltale film to prove it had been there. But even now it was fading.

A little, he mused, like men's lives.

Eagle-sharp, gray eyes peered out from beneath eyebrows that had become steadily shaggier over the course of seven decades.

He raised those cold, humorless eyes to regard the man standing nervously before him. The man who had brought him a report that he found to be far from satisfactory.

He took his time before he spoke, knowing that the longer he took the more nervous the spineless wonder before him became.

He enjoyed making those beneath him squirm. And they were *all* beneath him.

"And do we know where the good senator is now?" he asked in a steely voice that sent daggers of fear into the hearts of those lesser individuals.

The man who had been summoned to report did his best not to show fear. Displays of fear only served to enrage the venerable man who headed their small, elite society.

"He's staying at his estate. His son came the other day to help him mount a defense."

"Which son?" he questioned sharply.

"Dylan. The lawyer," the messenger added.

"It's not the courts he should be afraid of," the seated man commented, stating something they both knew to be true. The Society was far more powerful than any court because it was not governed by courts or by any extraneous rules.

Taking another sip of the thick, dark liquid in his glass, he let it slide down, savoring the 112-year-old cognac before speaking again.

"You know what to do. He needs to be made aware of the consequences—and reminded exactly who he is dealing with." The flat eyes darkened, sending a chill through the room. "Teach him a lesson."

"Yes, sir."

The first man left the room, all but bowing as he backed out slowly, never averting his face even as he crossed the threshold. It wasn't just a sign of respect. He knew better than to turn his back on the man in the winged chair. Men had lost their lives that way, dying with stunned looks frozen on their faces for all eternity. Dying because of sins they were not even aware of having committed.

There were always consequences when dealings with the man who presided over the Society went awry.

Chapter 13

The signals Dylan felt he was receiving from the woman who had become his constant companion this last week and a half were mixed, and because of that, he found them somewhat confusing.

In the evenings, after they had both put in long hours at his father's office, trying to pull in all the various pieces that comprised the current life of Senator Henry William Kelley, they could figuratively let their hair down with one another. It was then that they stopped being responsible, functioning adults searching for an elusive key that would unlock the mystery that surrounded this sudden exposé surrounding the senator.

Leaving all that behind, they turned into just two normal people, exploring the uncharted terrain of a brand-new relationship.

His evenings, Dylan thought as he looked across his father's antique desk and watched Cindy work her way through yet another file, were rich with foreplay, resplendent with starbursts of satisfaction and all-encompassing warmth. His evenings were filled with a comfortable afterglow.

But the days, he had discovered, were far edgier. They were filled with purpose and a feeling of racing against the clock for reasons that were both apparent and possibly not so apparent. It was during the days that he detected a difference in Cindy.

Oh, she was still sweet, still innocently thrilling, but at times he would look up unexpectedly and catch her watching him, as if she were waiting for something. During those moments, when he'd try to make eye contact, she would lower her own eyes and pretend to be taken with whatever it was that she was working on.

It had been that way almost from the beginning of their intimate relationship. Her thoughtful stares had grown more pronounced, more frequent. He found himself needing to know what was going on in her head, what was prompting those unfathomable looks.

Finally, he had to ask.

"What?" he prodded.

Startled, Cindy shook her head, as if he'd caught her by surprise and she had no idea what he was talking about. "What do you mean 'what?'"

He leaned back in his father's soft imported-leather chair, his eyes never leaving her face.

"Exactly that," he replied, then repeated, "What? Why are you looking at me as though you expect me to evaporate or just go up in smoke?"

"Oh." Now the question made sense. She supposed she had been staring, but she didn't think he'd noticed. She'd tried not to be obvious. "Not smoke," she corrected.

"Okay, you put a name to it." What she called it wasn't important. He wanted to know what was behind her looking at him like that. "What is it you're waiting for me to do?" he wanted to know.

Cindy pressed her lips together, debating between coming up with a white lie or telling Dylan the truth. But she'd never been good at lying, a fact that one of the other people in the office had pointed out was rather ironic, given that she earned her living working in the political arena.

"Leave," she finally said, running her tongue over her dry lips nervously the moment the word was out.

He didn't quite follow what she was saying. The obvious seemed too far out in left field, but he asked anyway. "You want me to leave?"

Her eyes widened like two morning glories at the first stroke of sunrise, completely captivating him and interrupting his train of thought. Reminding him how much he enjoyed making love with her. How much he wanted to do it *now.*

"No, oh God, no," Cindy cried.

All right, he was now royally confused. "Then what do you—?"

Taking a breath, Cindy tried again, striving to be clearer. "I'm waiting for you to leave. Expecting you to leave, actually," she clarified, her voice low. "Or change."

"Change," he echoed. "Into what?" he wanted to know. "Some kind of supernatural creature?" What *was* she talking about?

She knew this had to sound crazy to him. And then again, maybe he was just feigning ignorance. Despite everything that had happened between them and the incredibly fast rate at which it had happened, she was still afraid to let her guard down completely.

"Into someone else," she finally told him.

Now it was clear. And somewhat insulting, he thought. "Like your ex-husband." Dylan reined in his temper because she probably didn't even realize that something like that would bother him. But it did.

She nodded her head. "Yes." With effort, she tried to continue reading the file she was going through, but the words were all swimming before her, not making any sense.

Dylan straightened up and leaned in closer over the desk. He'd thought this was behind them. Obviously not. "Didn't we already have this discussion?"

Cindy pressed her lips together before raising her eyes again. "There's a difference between words and actions," she pointed out quietly.

"No argument." For a long moment, he said nothing as he quietly studied her. What did it take to convince her? "Have I acted like him?"

"Yes. The before version," she quickly qualified. "Only better."

Dylan built on what she gave him. "Have I done anything to make you believe that I'm going to shape-shift, or morph, or whatever you want to call it, into the monster that he ultimately became?"

"He wasn't exactly a monster," she quickly protested, not out of any sort of loyalty to Dean, but out of a desire to keep things completely honest. She didn't want to have Dylan thinking that she was given to wild exaggerations.

"He hit you, had sex with you against your will," Dylan pointed out, his face stony. "That makes him a monster in my book." And then he paused as he struggled to make sense out of this new puzzle he was faced with, far more personal than the one involving his father. "Okay, what's your definition of a monster?" he wanted to know.

She hesitated only for a moment, then decided that Dylan had been right to fix the label on her ex. Dean was a monster.

"Dean," she said almost in a whisper.

Dylan's eyes kept hers prisoner. He needed to see her eyes when she answered him. "But not me, right?"

Feeling like someone about to make her way onto a tightrope stretched across a chasm, she said, "No, not you." But then, she knew that if she wanted to be honest with him as well as with herself, she had to qualify her answer. "Yet," she whispered.

He was surprised as well as frustrated with her reply.

The beginning of a heated protest, born of impatience, was on the tip of his tongue, ready to emerge amid an explosion. But raising his voice, losing his temper, none of that was going to help gain Cindy's trust or put her at ease.

So he struggled and managed to keep his voice on an even keel.

"Not ever," he told her firmly, his eyes pinning her in place. "Got that?" he asked tersely. "Not *ever*. Not even when you drive me crazy and I lose my temper. None of that is an excuse or a justification for sub-human behavior, which was what your ex exhibited." Both hands pressed against the side of the old desk, he pushed the chair he was sitting in away from it. "I'm ready to call it a day, how about you?"

Cindy looked down at the file she'd been going through. She was almost finished with it and knew that she really shouldn't walk away until she'd gone through the entire thing. "I need another half hour or so."

He raised an eyebrow, instantly transforming

into his father's defense attorney right before her eyes. "Are you on to something?"

She really wished she was. Cindy shook her head. "No, I just want to be thorough before I put another file to bed."

His response surprised her. And pleased her as it went straight to her heart.

"I'd rather put you to bed," he told her. "With me next to you." Moving his chair back in for a moment, he turned the file she was working on toward him and thumbed through it. "Looking at that in the morning with fresh eyes might be a better idea, although I'm beginning to think that whatever we're looking for, we're not going to find it here. The old man's too good at hiding things," he said.

She didn't have the same opinion. Leaving the folder on top of the desk, she said, "And maybe sometimes a horse is just a horse."

Amusement highlighted his expression. "Is that some kind of folksy saying?"

Her back was instantly up, but she told herself to calm down. He wasn't being condescending, the way Dean had been every time she'd tried to make a point or have an intelligent conversation with him. She had to stop taking offense where none was intended.

"No," she told him, "I once heard a doctor say that. He told me that he had heard it in medical school. What it means in this case is that maybe there *is* no hidden meaning, no secret agenda. Maybe the senator just got one of his mistresses angry at him and she decided to get back at him by coming forward." She straightened the papers in the folder, then left it on the side of the desk. He was right. It could wait until morning. "Then the others followed, not wanting to be left behind in case there was something to be gotten out of this scandal—notoriety, their fifteen minutes of fame, I don't know," she admitted honestly. "The bottom line is that they all decided to follow suit and make a public confession. So, instead of one, there're now six mistresses."

"That's all well and good," he agreed, "as far as it goes. But what about these charges that the old man was stealing from the campaign funds in order to feather his so-called love nests? We're talking about potentially a great deal of money here." As of yet, a full tally hadn't been announced.

Cindy shook her head again, this time adamantly. "I don't buy it."

"Why not?" he wanted to know, curious about why she seemed so certain.

"No offense, but your family, thanks to your mother's father, has more money than God." To her, money had always meant being able to be comfortable. Sums of the kind that Dylan was probably accustomed to were something she couldn't begin to fathom. They were on par with the money used in a game of Monopoly: unreal. "There's certainly enough there for your father not to have to risk getting caught with his hand in the till."

Technically, she was right, but Dylan wasn't so sure about the reality of it. "My father has a huge ego. One that allows him to think he's entitled to do anything he wants to do."

Where could he have gotten that kind of an impression? The Senator Henry Kelley she knew was a kind man, a man of the people.

"No, he doesn't," Cindy insisted. She could see that Dylan was far from won over. "Maybe you don't know him as well as you think you do. The senator is *not* some egomaniac. Some-one gave you the wrong information about him," she told him.

"Maybe," Dylan allowed. Rising before something else came up, Dylan put his hand out to her. "Let's call it a night and not talk about my father anymore. The man's already taken up far more than enough of our time for one day."

Cindy smiled shyly as she rose, slipping her hand into his. She loved the way Dylan held her hand, as if there was a promise of more to come. Loved the way he made her feel. But at the same time, she couldn't completely shut out the growing fear that all this was just temporary, a smoke screen to throw her off from seeing things the way they actually were.

She was, she thought, just too happy. And happiness, she knew, had a way of abruptly disappearing without any warning.

Guiding her toward the hallway, Dylan paused to kiss her cheek. He could almost *see* the thoughts as they popped up in her mind.

"Stop waiting for me to grow fangs," he whispered into her ear. "It's just not going to happen."

She wanted to believe him. She *really* wanted to believe him. But she couldn't, not completely.

Once burnt, twice leery.

The old saying was all but burned into her brain, suddenly glowing brightly each time she thought she'd successfully eradicated it.

It refused to allow her to relax.

As had become his habit, Dylan swung by the family estate to check on his father and make sure everything was all right before going on to Cindy's apartment for the evening.

Business before pleasure, he thought, although, with Cindy continually championing his father's cause so passionately, Dylan had to admit he was beginning, ever so slowly, to change his perception not just of the situation but of the man as well.

Cindy believed in his father's innocence when it came to taking the campaign funds. She wasn't some empty-headed little bimbo his father had hired because of her looks. She was an intelligent, dedicated young woman. Cindy had proven to be more than capable.

She could not only handle the initial job she had been hired for with aplomb, in addition, she could juggle facts, figures and schedules for the senator, keeping on top of all of them, something that would have made a less capable person throw up their hands in utter despair and either quit on the spot, or weep.

She did neither.

And if *she* believed his father to be the victim of an intricate smear campaign, then maybe there was something to that. The key, as he'd already decided before, lay with the person or persons behind this onslaught of media blitz his father was caught up in.

Approaching the compound via the back entrance, Dylan called ahead to the private detective he'd temporarily hired as his father's bodyguard until he could get his father up to Cole and Montana. He knew better than to surprise the man and arrive unannounced. It was a good way to acquire an unwanted bullet in some part of his anatomy.

James McNeil met him at the back door. Just prior to opening the door, the private investigator disengaged the brand-new, complex security system that Dylan had insisted on having put in place by a firm he knew—and a man he trusted. The previous one that had been in place since his father had first become a senator presented absolutely no challenge to anyone the slightest bit seasoned in the "art" of breaking and entering.

While the new system was going in, he'd left a message for his mother on her cell phone, informing her of the change, although he sincerely doubted that she intended to visit the estate any time soon. At least, not as long as his father was here. But it was better to cover all the bases than to leave something to chance. He was nothing if not thorough.

"How's it going?" Dylan asked as the private

investigator, a deceptively mild-looking man—until one caught a glimpse of the weapon at his waist—stepped back to allow him access to the rear hallway.

"Nothing to report," James replied. He closed the door again and reengaged the security system in a matter of seconds. McNeil had brought in two of his agency's associates so that there would be someone wide-awake and alert at the estate at all times. "Other than your father going a little stir-crazy," he remarked.

His father was accustomed to coming and going when he pleased and being surrounded by fawning constituents and lobbyists. This had to be one hell of an adjustment for him, Dylan mused.

"Better that than being shot at," Dylan commented to the P.I.

McNeil looked at him dubiously. "You really think it was going to come to that?"

"I don't know," Dylan replied truthfully. "But I know that the old man did."

McNeil considered the answer, then shrugged. "Could just be a matter of paranoia."

"Could be," Dylan agreed. "But I figure it's better to be safe than sorry. If the old man's wrong and nobody's got him in their sights—" Dylan shrugged "—hell, he's just out some money. But if he's right and precautions weren't taken, well, being right then would be a pretty hollow victory."

Footsteps echoing on the gleaming travertine-tiled floor had McNeil raising a cautionary hand. The next moment, the tension abated as Hank joined them, his ever-present companion in his hand—a glass half-filled with something alcoholic in nature. In his utter boredom he was systematically going through his liquor cabinet one bottle at a time.

For a moment, he looked genuinely happy to see his son. Happy to see another face other

than the ones that surrounded him on a continuing, rotating basis.

"I thought I heard your voice," Hank said
just before he toasted his discovery and took
another sip from his constantly refilled glass.

The estate was far too large for his father
to have heard him from any of its wings. The
only logical assumption for Dylan to make was
that the senator had been shadowing McNeil.

"How are you doing?" Dylan asked his father, trying his best to sound as if the answer
truly mattered to him.

Hank looked at him over the rim of his glass.
"Is that a concern?"

He wasn't going to lie. He was far more his
mother's son than his father's. "That's a question," Dylan replied.

Hank laughed shortly. "How am I doing?"
he echoed. "Never thought something so big
could feel like the walls are closing in on me,"

the senator confessed. "Hell, I'm getting cabin fever," Hank complained.

"Well, it won't be for much longer," Dylan assured him.

Hank looked startled at the casual remark. "Why?" he demanded, leery and alert at the same time. "Are you calling off the dogs? No offense, McNeil," he tagged on, glancing at the P.I. on his right.

"None taken."

Dylan wasn't sure if his father was hoping for a positive answer—or fearful of one. "As soon as those bodyguards I hired arrive, you're being transferred."

Gage, it turned out, needed a couple more days to wrap up his present assignment. The fact that the bodyguard didn't just take off at the lure of a sizably larger paycheck spoke well of the man, even if it did heighten the anxiety factor, Dylan thought. He'd be greatly relieved once his father was safely hidden away in Montana. He knew that Cindy felt the same way.

"Transferred," Hank echoed. There was more than a little disdain in his voice as he said the single words. "From one prison to another, is that it?"

"Montana is far too wide open to be considered a prison, Dad," Dylan tactfully pointed out. "You need anything?"

Hank laughed shortly, his piercing gaze sweeping over both of the younger men. "Yeah, I need to get my old life back."

That wasn't his fault, Dylan thought, annoyed. Hell, he had better things to do than get bogged down, defending and protecting a father who, at best, could not have been referred to without the word absentee being involved.

"You should have thought about that before you started burning the candle at both ends," Dylan told his father. To his credit, McNeil acted as if he hadn't heard the exchange. Dylan knew that *nothing* got past the P.I., though.

He expected his father to argue with him. When he didn't, when he sighed and murmured, "I guess you're right," Dylan caught himself actually feeling sorry for the man.

More of Cindy's influence, Dylan realized.

He needed to get back to her. Needed to get back to the life-affirming aura she managed to generate without even thinking about it.

Discovering Cindy, he knew, was the best thing that had come out of this impossible little mini-drama he'd gotten pulled into.

"Hang in there, Dad. We'll get to the bottom of all this and things'll get better."

For a moment, heartened by the remark, the old Hank looked as if he was returning. "You said *we*," he pointed out.

He was about to say it was just a figure of speech, a slip of the tongue, but his father looked so happy Dylan couldn't bring himself to shoot the senator down.

"Yeah, I did. Well, if there's nothing else, I've got to get going." He looked at McNeil. "Call me if something comes up." Then, glancing over his shoulder, he said, "You, too," to his father.

He turned around and left, thus missing seeing the grateful smile pass over his father's lips.

Maybe in some wild, off-kilter way, this would all eventually work out, Hank thought as he watched his son leave. Moreover, in some perverted sort of fashion, this terrible situation had managed to bring him closer to his family again, a position he should have never vacated.

Hank stood regarding the dwindling contents of his glass. He knew that, for the most part, this was the alcohol talking. But he clung to it anyway.

He had to believe that by his pulling out, he

had caused the Society's planned assassination attempt against the president to be aborted.

It was all that stood between him and a soul-annihilating guilt.

Chapter 14

Senator Henry William Kelley's conscience, something that the women he charmed, the colleagues he conned and the associates he used to his advantage more times than they realized all said he didn't possess, was indeed alive and well.

Presently, it was chafing Hank because he hadn't done anything about the information he knew, in his heart, to be true. There was, in his opinion, a very good reason for his inertia: passing this information on to the proper authorities could very well get him killed.

And who was to say he would even be believed if he did step forward? Hank thought, pacing about the study like the caged lion he felt he had become. If that did turn out to be the case, if his report to the authorities was completely discounted, he would be surrendering what was left of his tattered reputation, not to mention very possibly his life, for absolutely no reason at all.

On the other hand, if he said nothing, there was the possibility that he would remain safe, being let off by the powers that be within the Society with no more than a few scares and threatening warnings that he was to continue keeping his mouth shut.

But if he said nothing, there was also the very real possibility that the country would be rocked by an unexpected, devastating tragedy.

The sudden, violent death of a world leader was not something that faded quickly from the public's mind like yesterday's headline. Its effects lingered at times for years, leaving an indelible mark on the country.

Hank knew that no one could actually accuse him of ever being a patriot, but he wasn't a traitor, either. That was why he'd backed out so quickly from the Society that had invited him in, flattering his ego, playing up his desirable connections. The moment the glad-handing had settled down and the far more serious underlying intent became evident, he had realized that he was in way over his head.

The Raven's Head Society wasn't some exclusive good ol' boys' club where members threw back large glasses of expensive liquor and stood around swapping stories of acquisitions and sexual conquests, each tale more fantastic than the last. It wasn't even an organization designed to bring about the propagation of money and power for the purpose of placing it in the hands of a chosen few—at least, it wasn't organized exclusively for *just* that purpose.

He shivered involuntarily as he thought of that room he had been brought into. The men who had gathered there had a crystal-clear vision of how they meant to arrive at their goal.

Hank stopped pacing and leaned against a bookshelf. He realized that his hand was shaking.

Goddamn it!

Hank put his other hand on top of the first, trying to still the tremor born of fear and indecision. His moral fiber might be flexible, but it didn't include permanently eliminating someone by design. He'd said as much. But the moment he'd protested, he'd immediately realized his mistake.

What he *should* have done was maintain his silence and then find a reason to disassociate himself from these people.

But the sheer horror of what he heard being

proposed had words springing to his lips before he could think to swallow them.

And now he was on the record as something less than a sympathetic friend to the powers seated within that dark, forbidding room.

He was fairly certain that the man at the center of the group had been the one to orchestrate this media circus that had suddenly sprung up around him. And he—or one of his minions—had to have engineered the baseless scandal surrounding the campaign funds.

While he was forced to own up to the mistresses—even though he would have hardly referred to the lot of them as that—he flatly and categorically denied taking so much as a single penny of the campaign funds for his own personal use. He didn't need to dip into the money that had been earmarked for his next run for the Senate. He had more than enough of his own.

A moot point now, Hank thought bitterly.

There was no way he was going to be able to clear his name sufficiently to get back into the political arena. He knew defeat when it stared him in the face.

The question still remained. What did he do? Go with his conscience or with his survival instincts? Which was the right move?

Right now, he was inclined to keep his mouth shut and pray that the plans he fervently wished he had not had the misfortune of hearing would be scrapped, if for no other reason than the fact that he was now in the wind.

Hank continued pacing about the room, wearing a path in the rug as well as in his soul.

"A picnic?" Dylan repeated, not quite sure he'd heard Cindy correctly.

It was the last day in September and he'd declared it an unofficial holiday, feeling that they both needed a little time off, especially since things were about to gear up as far as matters surrounding his father were concerned. He'd wanted to catch a little free time with Cindy before the pace picked up and became close to frantic.

They were in her apartment right now. He had come by to ask her what she wanted to do for the next few hours that didn't include being stuck at the senator's office, going through files until they were both ready to hurl computers across the room.

He looked at her now, his father's "Chief Staff Assistant," the woman he had come to care for so much in such an incredibly short amount of time. In a shade less than two weeks, he'd gone from a fairly contented, dedicated bachelor to a man who found himself entertaining definite thoughts of domesticity—and longing for it. Right down to caring for the baby Cindy was carrying.

It still stunned him every time he realized this was where his mind-set was these days.

He couldn't really trace how it had evolved, he just knew that it had. And that he was aware of feelings that he'd never dreamed he would *ever* experience.

He supposed he had his father's chaotic life to thank for that. Odd how things turned out.

"You really want to go on a picnic?" he asked her, trying not to sound amused, sensing that she would take offense and think he was laughing at her.

That too, was new to him, this sixth sense he'd developed when it came to matters involving Cindy.

Life was a mystery all right, he thought not for the first time.

Cindy already had the picnic basket packed with things she knew he enjoyed eating after paying attention to what he ordered when they ate out. Tucked in on top of the sandwiches and various other things was a tablecloth, checkered, in keeping with classic tradition, as well as all the accessories needed to make this picnic—a first for her—a pleasurable, intimate experience. Dylan had literally brightened her world and she wanted to do something nice, something fun, both for him and with him.

She had already gathered that his life was fraught with serious responsibilities and she wanted to be able to make him kick back, if only for a little while.

When he'd called to say they were going to take a few hours off from the investigation, she'd impulsively thought of a picnic. She'd never been on a picnic herself, but she'd always wanted to go on one. This seemed like the perfect opportunity to do something about it.

"Yes," she answered. "I think it'll be fun."

"Fun," he echoed, immediately thinking of ants, mosquitoes and grass stains. And then he grinned.

Oh, what the hell?

"Yeah. Sure. Why not?" he said gamely.

After all, he was the one who'd told her they were going to take a little free time today. He'd done all he could right now, pulled all the strings he had available to him to pull. Bart Holden and Gage Prescott, the bodyguards he'd hired, were on their way and would probably be arriving here within the day.

As for where his father was going to be staying for the indefinite future, he'd called Cole again to update his twin on what was happening on his end. Cole still sounded far from pleased about playing host to their father, but he hadn't said no, either, so, as far as he was concerned, that was all set.

The only impasse so far was that he still hadn't found out who had originally leaked the story about the mistresses—and the fabricated stories about the skimming of campaign funds for personal use—to the media. But he had his people out, digging, and he was still optimistic that he'd get to the bottom of all this.

And he had more than earned the right to take a little break and enjoy himself.

More than he already was, he amended, his grin growing wider. Connecting with Cindy had been an unforeseen, remarkable plus. A reward, he now thought, for a good deed, however reluctantly undertaken at first.

As he reached for the picnic basket to carry it to the car for her, the room suddenly darkened, as if someone had thrown a switch that knocked out all the lights. Except, this was the middle of the morning and there were no lights on to begin with.

Until a second ago, the sun had been shining brightly, providing all the illumination necessary for the apartment. Now the sun had apparently slipped behind a cloud. More clouds, dark and ominous, appeared, gathering together and filling the sky. A foreboding rumble came to announce the pending rain. And just like that, it wasn't pending anymore. It was pouring. In what seemed like a matter of moments, they had gone from a perfect early-fall morning to a day plucked out of an early southern California winter with all its dreariness.

Stunned, as if she couldn't believe the weather could change so radically, Cindy hurried over to the window and looked out. Huge raindrops were already pelting the glass.

The storm had come out of nowhere and was now drenching all of her plans. She sighed, resigned. "I guess we're not having a picnic after all."

Dylan immediately picked up on her tone. She sounded more than a little disappointed. For some reason, having this picnic was important to her. He didn't understand why, but the very fact that it was enough for him.

"Why not?" he asked her as he came up behind her.

She turned around slowly, acutely aware that her body was brushing up against his. Acutely aware as well of the electricity that sparked and shot through her from the barest of contacts, warning her that she was going to be absolutely *devastated* when Dylan left, or changed, or otherwise managed to terminate this magical state she now existed in.

She looked up at him. He actually looked serious. Was he? "Well, for one thing, sandwiches taste better when they're not consumed underwater."

"Good point," he laughed. "And, don't worry, they won't be."

A hint of a smile curved her lips as she looked at him uncertainly. "Are you going to tell me that you're the reverse of a rainmaker? That with a sweep of your hand, the right words and some kind of an incantation, you can make the rain stop? Magically?" she added, her eyes dancing.

God, but she looked adorable, he thought. He wanted to forget about the picnic, forget about everything but her and just spend the rest of the day making love with her. But he'd decided to make the picnic happen for her, so picnic it was.

"Nope, sorry," he told her. "Magic like that just isn't part of my repertoire."

"Then what...?" Out of guesses, her voice trailed off as she waited for him to clarify his meaning.

"We can have the picnic here," he told her, gesturing around the living room.

He *was* kidding. "Here?" she echoed, completely confused.

"Sure," he told her enthusiastically. "We can spread the tablecloth out on the rug, pretend the rug is really grass, and just go from there. Of course, there won't be any ants to deal with or any mosquitoes or flies to wave away, but I figure in the scheme of things, that's pretty much of a plus."

A little spark of enthusiasm reared its head

within her. She would have been the first one to admit that this was silly, but she found herself loving him more for indulging her like this. For being open to indulging her. No one had ever done that for her before.

"You're serious?" she asked Dylan incredulously.

"Absolutely." He raised his right hand as if taking a solemn pledge and crossed his heart with his other hand. "Why? Don't I look serious?" he asked, opening up the basket she'd packed and taking out the tablecloth.

She took hold of the tablecloth's other end, then backed away in order to help Dylan spread it out on the rug.

Cindy had to admit that she was still rather stunned that he was actually going to go through with this. She would have bet anything that Dylan would have said that pretending to this extent was something that children did, not adults.

He probably had no idea how much this warmed her heart, she thought. But she intended to show him. Right after they finished eating, she was going to express her gratitude to him the best way she knew how.

The tablecloth down, she knelt beside the basket and started taking out the food she'd packed as well as the two plates and two sets of utensils. Both were of the throwaway kind, but she'd selected a variety that looked like something a person would save to use again in the future.

Squatting down beside her, Dylan helped her empty the contents of the picnic basket, placing various items in the center of the tablecloth. There had to be a ton of food to choose from, he judged. Just how much did she think he could eat? Especially when his mind was definitely *not* on food.

"You really went all out, didn't you?" he

commented, shifting the empty basket over to the side.

Maybe she had gone a little overboard, she thought. But there was a reason for that. "I wanted my first time to be memorable."

He nodded. "Understandable. Every first time should be memorable." And then he replayed what she'd just said in his head. "Wait a second…you never went on a picnic before?"

"No," she answered quietly.

There were so many experiences common to the average childhood that she had completely missed out on because she had grown up in the modern equivalent of an orphanage rather than in a home with a family. She felt that somehow made her lacking. Did he see it the same way, she wondered.

For a moment, Dylan just looked at her thoughtfully. Without cracking a smile, he said, "Maybe I can call around to the local pet shops, see if I can scare up an ant farm for you." And then he grinned.

He was teasing her, she thought. And then she saw that he was actually reaching for her landline, about to pick up the receiver. Cindy leaned over and put her hand on top of his, stopping him.

"I think I'll pass on that if you don't mind. I have an imagination, and, all things considered, I can visualize them crawling around, thank you."

Dylan laughed, drawing his fingers away from the telephone receiver. "You talked me into it. Shall we?" he asked, taking her hand again. He drew her with him as he settled on the floor, sitting cross-legged.

Cindy sank down next to him rather than across from him. She savored the bit of sunshine she felt bursting inside her. She couldn't remember ever being this happy for this long.

She raised her eyes to his lips. They were still

curved and he seemed to be taking in her every move. "You're humoring me, aren't you?"

"I'm enjoying you," Dylan corrected. "And just for the record, I happen to think the idea of having a picnic is great. But it's not the grass or the ants that make a picnic. It's not even the food." He drew a little closer to her, feeling that same strong tug that he'd been experiencing almost from the beginning every time he was around her. His voice lowered a little bit as he said, "It's the company." His eyes were already caressing her, the way his hands itched to do.

He made her feel special, Cindy thought. More than that, he made her want to forget about the picnic and just be with him, make love with him, pretend that there was no tomorrow, no end of the rainbow waiting for her the way she knew in her heart that there had to be.

She just wanted to pretend that this was going to go on forever. That he was always going to be with her like this, and that there was no empty feeling waiting for her in the shadows, ready to swallow her up whole once he walked out the door for the last time.

Banking down her less-than-cheerful thoughts, Cindy ordered herself just to enjoy the moment.

Taking out two of the sandwiches she'd prepared, she held one in each hand and asked, "What would you like to have? Ham and cheese or turkey?" As she asked, she held each one up in turn.

"I think I'll pick—"

Dylan didn't get a chance to finish his sentence. Suddenly, there was the chilling sound of glass breaking as shards came flying at them from the direction of the window like tiny, jagged daggers slashing their way through the air.

Something else came flying as well. Whizzing so quickly that it didn't seem real.

Instinctively, Dylan pulled Cindy to him and threw his body over hers to protect her as more glass shattered and a second and then third cracking noise was heard above everything else.

"What *is* that?" Cindy cried, confused, too stunned and dazed to be as frightened as she could be. "Is that lightning shattering the window?"

He'd heard it enough times up in Montana to know that this wasn't lightning—or thunder.

"You can't aim lightning," he told her, raising his voice to be heard above the noise.

"Gunshots?" she cried, her eyes wide in disbelief. "Are those gunshots?"

And then, just like that, the noise stopped.

The rain was still coming down hard—and coming in, thanks to the broken window—but there were no more sounds of shattering glass, no more sudden menacing cracks or bullets whizzing by.

The silence could just be to lull them into a false sense of peace. He needed to check it out, but he wasn't about to take any unnecessary chances, especially not with Cindy here.

"Stay down," he warned Cindy, then crawled over to the sofa and pulled down one of the decorative pillows. Judging the trajectory of the last three bullets, Dylan tossed the pillow up in the air into what had been just moments ago the line of fire.

The pillow fell back to the ground, untouched. Whoever had been firing had stopped. For good?

"Stay down!" he ordered when he saw Cindy beginning to get up. The next moment, shifting out of the window's line of sight, Dylan slowly rose to his feet.

"What's going on?" she demanded, more angry than frightened.

"Not sure yet, but someone just played target practice with your windows," he told her, carefully approaching the damaged window from the side.

Following with his eyes the path the bullets had taken, he saw that all three had embedded themselves into the wall well above the back of the sofa. They were all much too high to have hit anyone but a tall basketball player.

"Dean," Cindy breathed. He saw panic flash in her eyes before she managed to shut it away.

"Your ex-husband?"

Numb, Cindy nodded. She started to feel sick.

Dylan cautiously moved over to where the bullets had hit the wall. "Is he a lousy shot?"

"No." As a matter of fact, it was just the opposite. "He had some medals he won in a competition when he was in the army reserves," she answered. "He was really proud of his marksmanship." Her mouth went dry. "He once said he could kill me from so far away, nobody would ever know it was him." Her eyes shifted to his. "Why do you ask?"

"Because whoever just fired those shots was either one hell of a lousy shot—which I'm inclined to doubt—or this was just meant as a warning." She needed reassurance, he could see that. "From what you told me, your husband isn't in control enough just to send you a warning."

Sitting out of the range of the window, Cindy looked small and lost. Dylan crossed to her and put his arms around her, doing his best to make her feel safe.

"This wasn't Dean," he told her. "It's going to be all right." His voice was low, soothing and filled with a conviction he didn't fully feel yet.

"Dylan." Shifting her cheek from his chest, Cindy raised her head to look up at him. She thought of the phone call at the restaurant. The one that had no one on the other end. "What's going on?"

He knew he had to be honest with her about this. She'd never really trust him if he wasn't.

With a frustrated sigh, he admitted, "Beats the hell out of me."

Chapter 15

If Dylan needed a reminder about how fragile life could actually be, he'd just got it.

Big-time.

The thought sent an ice-cold chill up and down his spine.

Over and over again.

He'd almost lost her. Lost the woman he realized that he loved before he ever had a chance to tell her—or fully acknowledge the fact to himself.

It was a couple of hours later and the situation—and what could have actually happened—was beginning to really sink in.

Coming to grips with the thought that Cindy could have been killed had him far more shaken up than he would have ever thought was possible.

Once he'd made certain that Cindy hadn't been hurt either directly or by accident—a ricocheting bullet was not unheard of and could have done as much if not more damage as one that had been aimed—Dylan had called the police.

A veteran patrolman had arrived within fifteen minutes of the 911 call and taken their statements. Once he'd been apprised of the situation and had looked over the damage to Cindy's apartment, he had called the desk sergeant at the precinct and requested that a detective immediately be dispatched to the upscale high-rise building.

The latter, a burly, rumpled man who looked as if he'd slept in his brown suit more than once when the occasion called for it, had taken a little longer to arrive. Mumbling something about "damn L.A. traffic," the man, Detective John Weller, examined what he could and then he in turn had called in a crime scene investigation unit. The unit, two men and one woman, proceeded to methodically go over the apartment with a fine-tooth comb, collecting evidence.

It felt as if this was going to take forever, Dylan thought. Or at least the better part of the afternoon. "Looks like we're not going to have that picnic today after all," he said to Cindy, desperately trying to keep things light. Knowing he wasn't really succeeding.

The look in her eyes when she turned toward him told him that she was doing her best to seem brave and in control. In reality, he knew she was struggling to keep from thinking about what *could* have happened.

With his arm still around her shoulders, she leaned her head into his chest. A host of protective feelings instantly sprang up within him, filling up every available square inch of his soul.

Dylan made up his mind.

"You're not staying here tonight," he told Cindy. When she looked up at him, he added, "You're coming with me."

"So you do think it was Dean." It was the only conclusion she could reach, given what he'd just said and his tone.

"No," he told her. "Actually I don't."

And he meant that. This incident didn't have the earmarks of something that had been undertaken impulsively. It seemed too planned out. And from everything Cindy had told him about her ex-husband, despite one verbal threat, for all intents and purposes he had disappeared once she'd had him served with both the restraining order and the divorce papers.

"But I just don't think you should be alone tonight with your imagination." He tightened his arm around her, feeling exceedingly grateful that she was unharmed. He nodded at the yellow tape that had been placed liberally around the area, separating the living room from the rest of the apartment. "And who knows how long this yellow obstacle course is going to be up, marking your living room as a crime scene."

Overhearing this, the tall, seasoned-looking woman in charge of the crime scene investigation told them, "We'll try to be as fast as we can, but we also need to be thorough." It sounded as if she'd said those exact same words countless times and they just automatically emerged somewhere during the first couple of hours of evidence-gathering and tagging.

And then she gave them a piece of information that wasn't automatic. "Whoever took those shots did it from that building."

The woman indicated the tall apartment building visible through the shattered glass.

Logically, it was the only explanation. The building, although by no means a high-rise, was the only one that was facing Cindy's window. Since she lived on the seventh floor, a shot from the building across the street—itself twelve stories high—was highly doable.

Cindy looked, but she made no effort to take even a single step closer to the window. She was struggling to keep her fear at bay, to keep it from paralyzing her. "Do you know which apartment?" she asked quietly.

The woman flashed a comforting smile at her. "Not yet. But we will," she added with confidence.

"I'd appreciate being informed the moment you know," Dylan told her.

Rather than answer, the crime scene investigator glanced at the detective, as if seeking confirmation of the request.

The man parked his pen between the pages

of his pad. "Who are you again?" Detective Weller wanted to know.

"Dylan Kelley," Dylan told him, even though he'd repeated his name each time a new wave of police personnel had entered the apartment. "I'm Senator Henry Kelley's legal counsel."

The last part was new information. He'd wanted to keep his father's name out of this if possible. The man didn't need any more notoriety, or for someone to begin to connect the dots, but it was obvious that this was now out of his hands. That being the case, he decided to use his father's name to his advantage for once. Especially since he was convinced that the shooting had something to do with his father's situation.

Weller looked more amused than surprised. "I see. Don't do things the easy way, do you, Mr. Kelley?" the detective chuckled. "Any relation to the senator?" he wanted to know.

At times it was hard to realize that not everyone was aware of the connection. It was, like it or not, a great part of everything he did. "He's my father."

"Oh." Weller looked genuinely surprised. "Sorry about that." He went back to making notes inside his worn pad.

Dylan wasn't sure if the detective was apologizing for his initially flippant line about not doing things easily, or for the fact he pitied him because Hank was his father.

In either case, Dylan decided it was best to leave the matter alone. "Do you need us here any longer?" he wanted to know, nodding at Cindy to include her in the question.

"No, I think I've asked just about everything I need to for now. Where can I get in touch with either of you if I need to?" Weller looked from one to the other, his expression fairly amicable.

Dylan reached for his wallet and took out one of the business cards. "May I?" he asked, raising his eyebrows and indicating the pen that the detective was currently holding.

"Sure. Here." Weller handed over the pen.

Taking it, Dylan wrote on the back of his card, then held it out to Weller. "That's my cell number. You can reach me any time."

Slipping the card into his stretched-out jacket pocket, Weller turned toward Cindy and asked, "And the young lady?"

"She'll be with me," Dylan assured him before Cindy had the opportunity to open her mouth.

"I see." Taking back his pen, the detective nodded knowingly.

"I will?" Cindy asked the moment the detective went back to confer with the patrolman who had been the first to arrive on the scene.

Dylan nodded. "I said you were coming with me, remember?" he reminded her. "Put some of your things into a suitcase and we can get out of here."

For a moment, she appeared undecided, then pivoted on her heel and went down the very short hallway to her bedroom.

"Next time you might try asking me instead of telling me," Cindy pointed out, tossing the words over her shoulder as she walked into her bedroom.

"Didn't want to risk an argument," he told her. Following her into her bedroom, the room that had been a witness to his reawakening as a man, he drew her into his arms without any preamble. Dylan looked down into her face. "Didn't want to risk you."

Cindy sighed. Damn but the man could be so romantic when she least expected it. "You certainly make it hard for a woman to argue with you."

"Good," he pronounced just before he kissed the top of her head.

Cindy grabbed his arm before he could step back. "What was that?" she demanded.

He looked at her uncertainly. Where was she going with this? "A kiss."

"Yeah—from a doting uncle, maybe." She frowned. They hadn't been together long enough for their relationship to devolve to this state yet. "That does not qualify as a kiss from a man to a woman unless one of them is on their deathbed."

He grinned at her. He had to stop treating her as if she was about to break, and he knew it.

"My error."

Taking her back into his arms, this time he kissed Cindy properly. Kissed her with all the feeling of a man who had a just been given one hell of a scare that the woman he loved could have been snatched away from him—permanently.

For a moment Dylan allowed himself to get lost in the folds of the emotions that the kiss had generated. Pulling back, because they were not alone and he really wasn't at liberty to indulge himself, he looked down into her face. And felt his heart swell. Again.

"Better?" he asked,

It was amazing what a calming and yet exhilarating effect his kiss had on her, what kinds of feelings it could stir up within her. There was no doubt in her mind that the touch of his lips against hers instantly made her feel better about everything, even though she knew that logically, nothing had really changed—other than a minor shifting of the earth beneath her feet.

"Better," Cindy replied with a wide, contented smile.

"Okay, let's get you packed up and get out of here," he said, "Before I'm tempted to forget about those people in the next room, close the door and have my way with you."

The smile crinkled the corners of her eyes. "Now for *that* I want a rain check."

"Absolutely," he promised.

* * *

Cindy was packed and ready to go less than twenty minutes later.

For the sake of simplicity, and just because he couldn't tolerate the idea of being separated from her just yet, Dylan proposed that they just use his car for now and come by later to pick hers up.

Feeling too shaken up to drive anyway, Cindy agreed without a protest. That in turn told him just how extremely upsetting the incident had been to her, despite the brave face she was putting on.

Taking the elevator all the way down to the subterranean third level, Dylan led the way to where he had parked his car earlier. Reaching it, he stopped dead.

There was a note trapped between his windshield and the windshield wiper that lay dormant against the glass. A quick glance at the cars on either side of his told Dylan him that the eight-by-ten white sheet of paper had not been distributed by some would-be entrepreneur trying to drum up business.

This was intended for him alone.

Someone had followed him here. How else could they have known where he had parked?

"What is it?" Cindy asked, seeing the look on his face.

"I don't know yet," he answered, trying not to alarm her. Taking out his handkerchief from his pocket, he used it to remove the sheet of paper and then turned it around.

On it, written in block letters with what looked like a permanent laundry marker were the words:

CONSIDER THIS A WARNING, KELLEY. BACK OFF. NEXT TIME, WE'LL AIM LOWER AND WE WON'T MISS.

On his own, he hadn't made any enemies of this caliber. And he was willing to bet that neither had Cindy. This had to do with his father.

Damn it, what the hell have you gotten your-self into, old man? And what have you gotten us *into?*

Taking his hand, Cindy drew it closer to her and looked down at the note he was holding. Dylan watched as her complexion became an even paler shade.

"Who wrote this?" she wanted to know, her voice low, tight.

"I don't know," he told her honestly. "It's not signed and nobody I know block-prints threats. It's got to have something to do with my father."

Cindy nodded, agreeing. "Are you going to turn that over to the police?" she wanted to know, nodding at the note.

That wasn't his first inclination. "Not yet. I want to ask my father about it."

"All right, then, let's go," she said as he unlocked his doors. Dylan slipped the note into a blue folder he had on the backseat, then placed her suitcase into his trunk. Shutting the trunk, he came around to the driver's side and got in.

"First I want to stop by the hospital E.R.," he told her, securing his seatbelt around him.

She was instantly concerned. "Why? Are you hurt? Why are you being so macho? You should have said something right away." Though they were both seated, she hadn't buckled up yet. Leaning over to his side, Cindy started tugging on his jacket, looking for some telltale trace of blood to give her a clue where his injury was. "Where did the bullet—?"

Dylan caught her frantic hands, stilling them. "I'm not hurt," he told her.

She didn't understand. He wasn't making any sense. "Then why do you want to go to the E.R.?"

He'd thought that would be obvious to her. "To get you checked out."

Cindy blew out an impatient breath and sat back in her seat, suddenly weary from all these sudden spikes of adrenaline that surged through her.

"I already told you. I'm fine. You covered me completely, remember?"

That was his point. "Exactly. I knocked you down." He could see she was about to protest again. "Remember, there's not just you to think of anymore. There's the baby, too."

Fleeting confusion gave way to understanding. Since she'd stopped throwing up, what with everything that had happened in these last two weeks she'd completely forgotten that she was pregnant.

Or maybe that was just wishful thinking on her part. Although, she had to admit, the resentfulness about the entire situation had faded, ushering in resignation in its place.

"It's not like you threw me off a second-story balcony," she pointed out. "I was already sitting on the floor when you pushed me down. Onto a rug," she emphasized. "The only way it could have been softer is if you'd thrown me into a nest full of feathers—or foam rubber."

She wasn't going to talk him out of it. "I'd still feel better if a professional looked you over."

A sensual smile curved her mouth as her eyes drifted over the length of him. "You're a professional," she said. "I'll let you look me over for as long as you want."

"Tempting as that offer is, I'm talking about a *medical* professional," he stressed.

She supposed he was right. She really didn't want to argue with Dylan. But one thing seemed to be very apparent to her. "You're a lot more concerned about this baby than I am."

She had it wrong. "I'm concerned about *both* of you," he corrected.

"Why?" she wanted to know.

Under the circumstances, this wasn't the time or the place he would have picked. Dylan shrugged it off for now. "Don't ask silly questions."

But she was determined to get an answer out of him. Needed to get an answer out of him. *Needed* to have something to hold on to.

"Why are you so concerned?" she pressed again.

She wasn't going to back off. He could see that.

"Because I love you," he all but shouted. "Okay?" Aware how loudly that had come out, he lowered his voice. "Because my heart stopped when I realized someone was firing at us. When I thought about what could have happened to you if the shots had been aimed lower. Or if I hadn't been there to get you down to the floor—"

"But the shots weren't meant for me," Cindy pointed out. "You said you thought it was about the senator, remember? And that note all but confirmed it."

There was a twist to this that had just occurred to him. "And you're the senator's Chief
Staff Assistant, remember? Whoever is behind
the shooting might have been looking to make
an example out of you to get to my father—
and to me." He found that really ironic, that
the same person meant something to both of
them. He couldn't remember the last time he
and his father had felt the same about *anything*.
"In effect, getting two birds with one stone."

Maybe she *had* hit her head without realizing it. Her brain wasn't processing information
quickly enough. His words came echoing back
to her. Startled, she needed him to repeat them.

"Back up a minute," she said, shifting in her
seat to get a better look at him. "You used the
word *love* a minute ago."

"I was wondering if you'd even heard me," he
told her. She'd passed over the crucial phrase
without a comment the first time around. It
made him think that she was politely trying to

ignore the way he felt about her. Because she didn't feel the same way.

Since she was asking him about it, he felt a glimmer of hope that he'd been wrong.

"Was that just a throwaway word?" Cindy asked.

He looked at her for a long moment, his silence saying things more eloquently than any words. "What do you think?"

"I think I'd like to hear an answer to my question—and no lawyer-speak, please," she requested. "I want to know if you actually meant what you just shouted at me."

He looked a tad apologetic. "I didn't mean to shout."

That wasn't the point she was seeking to clarify and he knew it. "You're being evasive."

No, he was being nervous, he realized, something he was relatively unaccustomed to being. Time to be straightforward, he told himself.

"Yes, I love you. And I want you in my life

on a permanent basis." He took a breath. "I want you to marry me. When you're ready."

It was the last sentence that made her eyes sting as tears suddenly gathered, threatening to spill out. Could someone possibly be this kind, this loving? Almost afraid to ruin the moment, she still had to ask, had to know. "And this baby I'm carrying, it doesn't make a difference to you?"

"Of course it makes a difference." He saw the glimmer of fear in her eyes. How was he ever going to make her understand? "I *like* the idea of having a family. And I want to be there with you every step of the way with this child. I want to be there when the baby's born, I want to be the one who cuts the cord."

She wanted this, oh God, how she wanted this, but she was more than a little afraid to reach for it. Afraid that if she closed her fingers around it, there would be nothing but air in her hand.

"But the baby's not yours," she said quietly. Would he grow to hate the child, to see the embodiment of her ex-husband in the child's features? Would it ultimately wind up tearing them apart?

He could only smile at her. She still didn't get how he felt. But she would. "Haven't you heard? Possession is nine-tenths of the law."

Cindy wiped away the tears that insisted on sliding down her cheeks, the tears that refused to be blinked back. A relieved smile curved her mouth. "I should know better than to try to argue with a lawyer."

"That's right, you should." He started up his car. "Now let's get you to the hospital." Looking over his shoulder for any stray vehicle pulling out or coming in, Dylan began to back out of the guest parking space.

"I love you, too."

He slammed on the brake much the way he felt his heart had just slammed against his rib cage. Who would have thought that such a little word contained so much firepower?

"What did you just say?"

"I said I love you, too. I just thought you should know. I was just afraid to say it or feel it," she confessed, "because…" She couldn't bring herself to put it into words. "Well, you know why."

He didn't want her going through any extra angst on his account, so he didn't challenge her dogged misconception. Eventually, she'd learn he wasn't her ex. "Yes, I know."

He started to back the car up again.

"But you're not going to become like him— like Dean—" she forced herself to say her ex-husband's name "—are you?"

Did she even have to ask? But he saw by the expression on her face that she did. Whatever it took, he decided. He was going to be there for her no matter what. "Nope. All I want to do is spend the rest of my life making you happy."

"Stop the car," she ordered.

Concerned, Dylan immediately stopped backing out again and pulled up the hand brake, putting the car into Park. "Are you feeling sick?"

She shook her head. "No, I just don't want you slamming on the brakes again when I tell you."

He had no idea what she was referring to. She'd already rocked his world by telling him she loved him. "Tell me what?"

Her eyes were smiling at him as she uttered the single word. "Yes."

He approached the declaration cautiously, as if she were a rare bird that, feeling threatened, might take flight at any second. He didn't want her to feel pressured to accept his proposal before she was absolutely ready. Now that he had found her, he was willing to wait for her.

"Are you telling me that you're willing to marry me?" he asked.

"Willing, ready and able," she added. "Just name the time and the place."

That was something to be decided by both of them after careful thought and a long discussion. At this moment, it was enough just to hear her agree to be his wife. "Right now, all I want to do is kiss you."

"That can be arranged." She leaned into him. "See? Aren't you glad I told you to stop the car?"

"You have no idea," he told her, enveloping her in his arms just before he brought his mouth down on hers. And if the automatic transmission stick happened to get in the way, neither one of them really noticed. Or cared.

Epilogue

The shooting at the high-rise apartment made the afternoon news.

Hank had been restlessly flipping channels when the words "sniper or snipers unknown" literally seemed to leap up at him, instantly seizing his attention.

His hand frozen on the remote, he stopped breathing. And listened.

And grew ghostly pale.

The police, according to the reporter, a young woman with flawless skin and perfect hair who had yet to see the inside of thirty—or real life for that matter—had no clue as to a motive or who the gunman or gunmen might be.

They didn't know, but he did, Hank thought.

He wasn't completely certain as to the actual man who'd been behind the trigger doing the shooting. But he knew without a doubt who was behind the shooting. Who had undoubtedly ordered it.

The same man he was running from.

The news piece ended and, for balance, was followed by a fluff piece about the local zoo's unexpected baby boom.

Hank didn't hear a word. Preoccupied, he crossed to the bar to pour himself a drink. Granted, it was early, but he desperately needed something to steady his nerves. Something to numb the growing, encroaching panic he felt sweeping through him.

Maybe if he talked to the man at the Society's head, promised that he would take what he had heard at that one meeting to his grave without saying a single word to anyone—

His hand shaking, he spilled some of the aged whiskey he was pouring onto the bar. Cursing, he left the telltale pool of alcohol where it was and moved away from the bar.

If he put that idea in their heads, if he said that about taking the secret to his grave, Hank thought, they'd probably *put* him in his grave within twenty-four hours—if it took that long—so he could keep his word.

He threw back the drink and went to pour himself another.

When he was still a kid, he had liked watching classic comedies that turned up on TV in the wee hours of weekend mornings. For a time, he'd been obsessed with Laurel and Hardy. A catchphrase often uttered by the beleaguered heavyset Oliver Hardy was, "Well, here's another nice mess you've gotten me into." He always said it when things began to fall apart.

He couldn't say that to anyone, Hank thought. Because in this case, he had no one to blame but himself. He and he alone was responsible for the mess he was in.

There was absolutely no comfort in knowing that. Moreover, if he wasn't careful, others around him would pay for his mistake, for his incredibly poor lack of judgment.

According to the news story, Dylan and Cindy had come close to being casualties of the unknown sniper. That was all his fault.

Oh God, he wished he could go back in time. He would never have walked in on that wretched meeting. Never have let his ego lead him on this wrong path.

The phone rang.

Startled, he almost dropped his second drink. As it was, he spilled some more, this time on the rug.

That was going to stain. He was going to have to mention it to the housekeeper, Hank thought dully as he reached for the receiver.

He placed the receiver to his ear and cautiously said, "Hello?"

"Dad?" He instantly recognized Lana's voice, despite the fact that it sounded unusually shaky. "Daddy?"

His hand tightened on the receiver. She was frightened, he could hear it. Something was very, very wrong. He felt sick to his stomach.

"Lana? Lana is that you?" The sick feeling began to spread. *Let her be safe.* Please, *let her be safe.* "Honey, what's wrong? What's happened?" he demanded, fear all but gutting him.

"They have me, Daddy. These men, they were on my train. I think they drugged me." Everything was foggy. "I don't know where I am." Her voice broke. "They told me that if—"

Abruptly, she stopped talking.

Panic seized him. "Lana? Lana, what's happening?" Hank cried. The drink had slipped through his numb fingers, falling to the floor. Its contents soaked into the beige rug. "Are you all right? Talk to me! What's happening?" he demanded, angry and afraid at the same time, his imagination running away with him, instantly creating horrible scenarios.

"Nothing, you had better hope," a deep voice informed him. It was the voice that now haunted his nightmares, causing him to wake up in a cold sweat, shaking. "Listen carefully, Senator. As long as you keep your mouth shut, she'll be fine. If you talk to anyone about what you know—*anyone*—well, I don't think I have to tell you what's going to happen, now, do I?"

"Don't hurt her. Please don't hurt my daughter," Hank begged.

The words were measured, leisurely strolling out one by one. "That is entirely up to you."

The click echoed in his ear.

"Hello? Hello!" Hank shouted into the phone, but the connection had been terminated.

Distraught, he flung the cordless receiver across the room. It hit the hall, creating a dent and leaving a dark mark.

Almost as if in response to the thud, there was a knock on the door behind him. And then, the visitor obviously not waiting for permission to enter, the door began to open.

His heart pounding, Hank swung around, fully expecting this to be his last few moments on earth. They'd found him, the Raven's Head Society's henchmen, they'd found him.

It was all over.

He numbly watched as the private investigator Dylan had hired to stay at the house as his temporary bodyguard walked into the room. There was another man with him, a tall, steely, hard-looking stranger with eyes that were cold and flat.

Hank knew he was looking into the eyes of a hired killer.

His executioner.

The stranger must have taken McNeil prisoner, Hank thought. The man didn't looked distressed, but then McNeil wouldn't. Death was always in the mix for people like that.

But it wasn't supposed to be for men like him, Hank thought frantically. "Are you here to kill me?" he asked the stranger, a tremor in his voice.

What might have passed for amusement fleetingly creased the stranger's mouth before it returned to being humorless in the next moment.

"No," he replied in a voice that displayed no emotion. "I'm here to protect you. I'm Gage Prescott, your new bodyguard. Dylan sent for me."

* * * * *